Prologue

October 5, 1813

Ontario

The Shawnee chief Tecumseh is killed today in a battle with American troops in Moraviantown, 60 miles east of Detroit. Born before the United States declared independence, Tecumseh had spent his adult life militarily and diplomatically resisting the country's expansion onto Native American lands. A persuasive orator, he'd traveled widely, forming a Native American confederacy and promoting intertribal unity.

In 1808, he and his brother Tenskwatawa, known as the Shawnee Prophet, had established Prophetstown, a village in present-day Indiana. Prophetstown grew into a large, multi-tribal community with Shawnees, Potawatomis, Kickapoos, Winnebagos, Sauks, Ottawas, Wyandots, and Iowas. American forces led by General William Henry Harrison, fresh from the battle of Tippecanoe, destroyed the village in 1811. Partly on the shoulders of the campaign slogan "Tippecanoe and Tyler Too," Harrison later became the ninth U.S. president.

3

At 31 days, his presidency was the shortest in American history.

A British and Indian force took a few American troops prisoner during a battle shortly after Prophetstown's destruction. When a group of Indians began killing the prisoners, Tecumseh stopped the slaughter. According to one historian, "Tecumseh's defense of the American prisoners became a cornerstone of his legend, the ultimate proof of his inherent nobility."

His nobility was not reciprocated. After the Moraviantown battle, American soldiers scalped Tecumseh and peeled off sections of his skin as souvenirs.

February 8, 1820

Lancaster, Ohio

A son is born today to Charles Robert Sherman, a justice on the Ohio Supreme Court, and he includes the name Tecumseh in his son's. Why he admired the name is not recorded, but its Native origin apparently evoked no sense of fraternity in the son. In addition to his prominent role in the Civil War, General William Tecumseh Sherman supervised wars against native Americans, evicting them from the lands they'd called home for centuries.

4

Sherman's March to the Sea

Crushing the South's will to fight is Sherman's ultimate goal as his army marches from Atlanta to Savannah. The objective is pursued not just by victory in battle, but by widespread destruction, with particular focus on military and transportation facilities. Rail lines are torn up, many rails permanently ruined by being heated, then twisted into forms that became known as "Sherman's neckties." The neckties are often wrapped around trees and telegraph poles.

Orders issued at the campaign's onset illustrate Sherman's goals and the army's tactic of sustaining itself by foraging from local residents. Many of the foraging crews, unofficially known as "bummers," don't abide closely to the orders, often taking blankets, clothing, silverware and other valuables. If residents are uncooperative, sometime regardless of their cooperation, their homes are burned.

From those orders:

... IV. The army will forage liberally on the country during the march. To this end, each brigade commander will organize a good and sufficient foraging party, under the command

of one or more discreet officers, who will gather, near the route traveled, corn or forage of any kind, meat of any kind, vegetables, corn-meal, or whatever is needed by the command, aiming at all times to keep in the wagons at least ten days' provisions for the command and three days' forage. Soldiers must not enter the dwellings of the inhabitants, or commit any trespass, but during a halt or a camp they may be permitted to gather turnips, apples, and other vegetables, and to drive in stock in sight of their camp. To regular foraging parties must be intrusted the gathering of provisions and forage at any distance from the road traveled.

V. To army corps commanders alone is intrusted the power to destroy mills, houses, cotton-gins, &c., and for them this general principle is laid down: In districts and neighborhoods where the army is unmolested no destruction of such property should be permitted; but should guerrillas or bushwhackers molest our march, or should the inhabitants burn bridges, obstruct roads, or otherwise manifest local hostility, then army commanders should order and enforce a devastation more or less relentless according to the measure of such hostility.

VI. As for horses, mules, wagons, &c., belonging to the inhabitants, the cavalry and artillery may appropriate freely and without limit, discriminating, however, between the rich, who are usually hostile, and the poor or industrious, usually neutral or friendly. Foraging parties may also take mules or horses to replace the jaded animals of their trains, or to serve as pack-mules for the regiments or brigades. In all foraging, of whatever kind, the parties engaged will refrain from abusive or threatening language, and may, where the officer in command thinks proper, give written certificates of the facts, but no receipts, and they will endeavor to leave with each family a reasonable portion for their maintenance.

Dolly Lunt Burge was the widow of Thomas Burge, a plantation owner and gentleman of the Old South. Her diary relates the impact of Sherman's orders on ordinary Southerners in his army's path.

November 16, 1864

On our return from Covington we rode through Madison, Old Dutch pulling the buggy. It was a pleasant ride as it was a delightful day, but how dreary looks the town! Where formerly all was bustle and business, now naked chimneys and bare walls, for the depot and surroundings were all burned by last summer's raiders. Engaged to sell some bacon and potatoes. Paid seven dollars a pound for coffee, six dollars an ounce for indigo, twenty dollars for a quire of paper, five

7

dollars for ten cents' worth of flax thread, six dollars for pins, and forty dollars for a bunch of factory thread.

On our way home we met Brother Evans accompanied by John Hinton, who inquired if we had heard that the Yankees were coming. He said that a large force was at Stockbridge on its way to Savannah. We rode home chatting about it and finally settled it in our minds that it could not be so. Probably a foraging party.

November 18, 1864

Uneasy yesterday and today. When I went outdoors I saw large fires like burning buildings. The neighbors say it's a large force moving very slowly. What shall I do? Where go? Am I not in the hands of a merciful God who has promised to take care of the widow and orphan?

Spent part of the day packing up my and Sarah's clothes. I fear that we shall be homeless.

The boys tell me the Yankees camped at Mr. Gibson's last night and are taking all the stock in the county. They took my mules and theirs and Elbert's forty fattening hogs to the Old Place Swamp and turned them out there.

November 19, 1864

Slept in my clothes last night, as I heard that the Yankees went to neighbor

Montgomery's on Thursday night at one o'clock, searched his house, drank his wine, took his money and valuables, and drove off all his stock.

This afternoon, standing on the porch, I saw some bluecoats coming down the hill. I hastened back to my frightened servants and told them that they had better hide. Like demons the Yankees rushed in to my yards. To my smokehouse, my dairy, pantry, kitchen, and cellar, like famished wolves they came, breaking locks and whatever was in their way. The thousand pounds of meat in my smokehouse was gone in a twinkling, my flour, my meat, my lard, butter, eggs, pickles, wine, jars, and jugs, all gone. My eighteen fat turkeys, my hens, chickens, and fowls, my young pigs, were shot down in my yard and hunted as if they were rebels themselves. Utterly powerless I ran out and appealed to a colonel.

"I cannot help you, Madam; it is orders."

As I stood there they drove away old Dutch, my dear old buggy horse, who carried my beloved husband so many miles, and who would so quietly wait at the block for him to mount and dismount, and who at last drew him to his grave; then came old Mary, my brood mare, who for years had been too old and stiff for work, with her three-year-old colt, my

9

two-year-old mule, and her last little baby colt. There they go! There go my mules, my sheep, and, worse than all, my boys! (Her slaves.)

They were forcing my boys from home at the point of the bayonet. One, Newton, jumped into bed in his cabin, and declared himself sick. Another crawled under the floor, but they pulled him out, placed him on a horse, and drove him off. Mid, poor Mid!

My poor boys! My poor boys ! What unknown trials are before you! How you have clung to your mistress and assisted her in every way you knew. Never have I corrected them; a word was sufficient. Never have they known want of any kind. Their parents are with me, and how sadly they lament the loss of their boys. Their cabins are rifled of every valuable, the soldiers swearing that their Sunday clothes were the white people's, and that they never had money to get such things.

Poor Frank's chest was broken open, his money and tobacco taken. He has always been a money-making and saving boy; not infrequently has his crop brought him five hundred dollars and more. All of his clothes and Rachel's clothes, which dear Lou gave before her death and which she had packed away, were stolen from her. Ovens, skillets, coffee-mills, of which we had three, coffee-pots - not one have I left.

Sifters all gone!

Sherman himself and a greater portion of his army passed my house that day, not only in front of my house, but from behind; they tore down my garden palings, made a road through my back-yard and lot field, driving their stock and riding through, tearing down my fences and desolating my home when there was no necessity for it.

Such a day, if I live to the age of Methuselah, may God spare me from ever seeing again!

As night drew its sable curtains around us, the heavens from every point were lit up with flames from burning buildings. Dinnerless and supperless as we were, it was nothing in comparison with the fear of being driven out homeless to the dreary woods. Nothing to eat! The colonel had left me two men as guards, but they were Dutch, and I could not understand one word they said. When they found I had no supper for them, they left.

The next day, some of my women gathered up a chicken that the soldiers shot yesterday, and they cooked it with some yams for our breakfast. By ten o'clock Sherman's army finally all passed.

November 21, 1864

We had the table laid this morning, but no bread or butter or milk. What a prospect for delicacies! My house is a perfect fright. I had

11

brought in Saturday night some thirty bushels of potatoes and ten or fifteen bushels of wheat poured down on the carpet in the ell. Then the few gallons of syrup saved was daubed all about. The backbone of a hog that I had killed on Friday, and which the Yankees did not take when they cleaned out my smokehouse, I found and hid under my bed, and this is all the meat I have.

The Story

Frank goes to War

July 11, 1863

Frederick, Maryland

A year before Sherman torches Georgia, twenty-year-old Frank Archer and his neighbor Samuel Rogers watch as segments of the Union Army pass through Frederick. Some are heading toward confrontation with the Confederates near Williamsport. Others—bandaged, bloody, limping after the huge battle at Gettysburg—collapse in makeshift hospitals in the town's churches and other buildings. During the course of the war, over ten thousand wounded are housed in Frederick.

Frank and Samuel live near Buckeystown, four miles south of Frederick, have been friends all their lives. Frank works alongside his father on their forty-acre farm, growing corn and other crops. At sixteen he leaves school to work the farm full-time. He enjoys the work, loves outdoor life, hunts the fields and woods with Samuel in his spare time.

A year later, General Jubal Early's Confederate corps defeats a hastily organized Union force under Gen. Lew Wallace at the Monocacy River, then camps in Frederick. Supposedly because the town's women booed Stonewall Jackson's troops as they passed through the previous year, Early gives the city a choice: pay a ransom of $200,000 or be burned. Local banks pay the fee with cash—almost $4 million in today's dollars—in buckets.

Frank is no longer in Buckeystown when Early empties the Frederick banks. Two months earlier, Congress had passed the first American conscription act, and Frank and Samuel are drafted into the army. After training, their regiment becomes part of the Army of the Cumberland's XIV Corps.

The Corps' campaign leads Frank to circumstances and meetings that will give meaning to the rest of his life.

November 25, 1863

Chattanooga, Tennessee

Sherman's XIV Corps is instrumental in the assault on Missionary Ridge, a hill near Chattanooga. Though the ridge is eventually captured, the attack fails.

As Frank, a corporal, led his squad below the ridge, a Confederate bullet ripped through his hand. He fell on his side, blood spurting from a torn vein, drenching the arm of his uniform.

Samuel fell alongside him and pulled him into a shell crater. "We gotta stop that bleeding."

Using his bayonet, he cut a strip from his trouser leg, wrapped Frank's wrist and twisted the cloth tight. The bleeding stopped. "Think that's got it. How do you feel?"

"Well, it hurts, but I think I can keep goin'. Where's the rest of the squad?"

"They're above us on the hill."

A mortar shell exploded a dozen yards from them, shaking the ground and sending shrapnel screaming above the muddy crater. They fell flat to the bottom of the hole, pressing tight against the dirt, holding their ears. Another, then another, then another shell landed close by, jarring the earth. Lying on his side, Frank watched Samuel's face, just inches from his own, jerk with each explosion, his eyes slamming shut. Dirt blasted into the air fell on them.

It seemed to Frank the barrage would never quit, but finally it slowed, came to a stop.

Samuel wiped dirt from the side of his face. "You think that's it?"

Frank saw Samuel's mouth move but heard nothing. He pointed at his ear, yelled, "What?"

Samuel yelled back, "You think they're done?"

"Yes."

Samuel lifted his chest out of the mud and looked over the crater's edge, then back at Frank.

"Are you okay? How's your hand?"

He bent over Frank's hand. "It's bleeding again, needs to be tighter." He reached into a shirt pocket and pulled out a spoon. "This'll do it."

He slid the spoon under a loop of the cloth on Frank's hand and turned it, twisting the improvised tourniquet tighter. The blood slowed. "I think that's got it."

"What?"

Samuel yelled, "I said that's got it! And luck's with you. That's my lucky spoon, been eating with it ever since this damn war started! How do you feel?"

"Guess I'm okay." He tried to sit up, but his head spun. He fell back in the mud. "Just a bit dizzy."

"You lie here a bit, I'm gonna see if the squad's okay."

Samuel crawled over the edge of the shell crater. Frank lay his head back, his hat sinking into the mud. The air stank of gunpowder and explosions. Streams of smoke drifted over the hole. His wrist felt like the tourniquet was crushing it, and his hand hurt like hell.

He heard the whistle of an artillery shell, then its blast. "The bastards!"

He rolled onto his stomach, inched his way up the crater's side and peered over edge. Samuel lay ten feet away, his body stretched on its back. The right shoulder of his uniform was shredded, the right side of his face was a mass of bloody flesh, the white of his cheekbone against his nose.

"Oh Jesus, oh Jesus, oh Jesus, no!" He lurched to his feet, staggered to Samuel, fell beside him and shook his shoulder. "Samuel, Samuel!"

Groans and coughing bubbled through Samuel's blood-filled mouth. His right eye was shredded. Open wide, his left looked into Frank as if asking a question. His left cheek twitched. He coughed again. The twitching stopped, the bubbling stopped.

His eye stayed wide open.

Frank wobbled to his feet. "Medic! Medic!" The dizziness slammed back into him, he fell and everything turned to black.

****

Frank's eyes opened slowly. Above him, coming in and out of focus, was a brown flatness. It was fuzzy, then sharp, streaked with dirt, and he realized it was the faded canvas of a tent ceiling. He raised his head. A row of cots filled with men stretched on one side of the tent. He too was on a cot, its wooden frame hard against his calves where they stretched beyond its foot.

I'm alive. I'm in a hospital.

He laid his head back and tried to remember. The ridge, the

16

shells landing around them, his hand. He raised his right arm. It was swathed in bandage up to his elbow. It hurt a lot.

Samuel, he'd been with Samuel in a shell crater and ... . He saw Samuel's ruined face, Samuel's eye, open, looking into him. Then he remembered it all.

That evening a doctor and two nurses made their way along the row of hospital cots, stopping at each, some briefly, some longer. As they moved toward him, he could hear some of their conversation.

"This bandage is soaked, it should be changed,."

"Call an orderly and clear this bed. He's gone."

"That leg's not looking good, he has to go back into surgery."

"How are you feeling this evening, son? Good, good, you should be back on your feet soon."

Beyond the bandaging and the pain, Frank knew nothing about his hand. When the doctor reached his bed, he asked.

"It's not bad son, but you did lose two of the fingers. They were badly mangled, so I amputated them. But it should heal up nicely, I used some of the extra skin from your hand to cover the amputation. You just need to take it easy, rest it, and listen to everything the nurses say. You'll be ready to rejoin your unit in a month or so."

Ready to rejoin my unit. Really?

The doctor reached into his pocket and brought out a spoon. "This was the handle of the tourniquet on your wrist when you were brought in here. That tourniquet may well have saved your life."

November 28, 1863

> Discharged from intensive care and assigned quarters with other recovering wounded, Frank walks through the Missionary Ridge grave site looking for

17

markers for his squad. There are thousands of graves, rows and rows of dirt mounds covering shallow trenches.

There are few markers, mostly officers, their names scratched on barrel staves or other boards stuck in the dirt. Rain has washed part of the dirt from some graves. Arms and legs protrude.

My god, what a price we've paid. What a price! And just what is it we've bought? The duty of those of us still alive to fight more battles, to kill more people? To see more of our friends and countrymen die?

He finds no marker for Samuel or anyone else from his

squad.

A week into his recuperation, his commanding officer, Colonel O'Reilly, called him to Corps HQ.

"Corporal Archer, it's come to our attention that you did a fine job of leading your squad during the recent battle. Very sorry to see you were wounded during that action, but you're obviously recovering well. In recognition of your leadership, the army is hereby awarding you a brevet commission. You are now Lieutenant Archer."

"Thank you very much sir, I'm not sure that I did anything out of the ordinary."

"Reports tell us otherwise. Congratulations, Lieutenant. Report to the Quartermaster's office for your uniform and insignia."

Frank saluted and left, puzzled.

I don't understand. Can't think of anything I did that was remarkable, just did what I could to have the squad fight as a squad. And my hand got blasted way before the battle was over, after that I didn't do anything at all.

What he didn't know was that four of the regiment's lieutenants had died during the battle.

A month after Missionary Ridge, he rejoined his unit as it began the march to Atlanta.

December 17, 1864

Archer's company is three miles north of Savannah, slogging through the marshes on the west side of the Savannah River. The river's floodplain is flat and broad, three miles across,

19

latticed with creeks and patches of oak trees, many dead and fallen. Cypresses rise from the marsh, their buttressed trunks surrounded by "knees," some hidden beneath the water, some reaching several feet above it. The men often wade in water to their waists, sometimes in mud approaching their knees. The water is red-black, pollen and dead grass swirled on its surface. Despite the season, mosquitoes are biting and poisonous snakes, particularly cottonmouths, are common. Since passing Milledgeville, they've seen no rebels. Occasionally they hear shots from the direction of Savannah. but otherwise the only sounds are the calling birds, the men's grunting and cursing, and the sound of their boots sucking out of mud.

Private Stephen Martin tripped over a submerged cypress knee and fell forward, the butt of his rifle stock burying in the mud. He stood up. The stock and his elbows had kept his face out of the mud, but the front of his uniform was coated and dripping. He wiped some of the mud off with the side of a hand and called to Archer, a dozen yards to his right.

"Lieutenant, couldn't ya have gotten us assigned up there on the ridge?"

"Well, Martin, I tried, but the colonel said he needed his toughest troops down in the bottom. Guess our reputation has some disadvantages."

"So if we we're crappy fighters we get to walk up on the

ridge?"

"There's no guarantee. Maybe he woulda said crappy fighters get rewarded by walkin' in the mud."

"That don't make much sense. I mean, walkin' in this shit, is it punishment or a reward?"

"He's the colonel, Martin. Take your choice."

The company emerged from a patch of live oak, Spanish Moss draped from its branches, mistletoe bunched in its tops, onto the bank of a winding creek. Across the creek was a strip of marsh grass, then more scrub trees.

Archer called, "Okay, Martin, you're in luck. We need to know how deep that crick is before we cross it. Let us know."

"Aw, Lieutenant!"

"Look at it this way, you'll be first to get that mud off."

Martin grimaced, walked to the creek bank.

"Hey, look at this water. It's real dark, almost like blood. Shit, is this from our guys?"

Archer walked to the bank of the creek. "No, it's not blood, least not most of it. It's what the rain does when it sinks down into the marsh, it washes out coloring from the dead plants and stuff. It's dead plants, not dead guys."

Martin edged his way into the reddish-black water, holding his Spencer over his head. In the center of the creek the water barely reached his waist. He swapped his carbine from one hand to the other, using the free hand to sluice mud from his uniform. The rest of the company waded in, some bending to wash mud off.

Archer was among the first to clamber to the opposite bank. The flood plain narrowed here, and the ridge, covered with trees, rose in front of them.

"Okay guys, easy duty now. You're all clean."

Martin slapped at his neck. "Yeah, with the mud off the skeeters got easy eatin'."

At the edge of the treeline a piece of cloth fluttered.

21

Private Kenneth Cleary called to Archer. "What's that, Lieutenant?"

"Can't tell. Maybe a flag." He waved an arm, pointed at the cloth. "Keep your eyes open, guys."

The company moved carefully toward the trees.

"Cleary, you take point."

The company kneeled and watched as Cleary moved to point. He kneeled, then dashed a few yards, then kneeled again, then dashed. Except for frogs croaking, there was no sound but his boots crunching the stiff grass.

After a few minutes he called back. "It's okay. He's dead."

The company clustered around a Confederate battle flag, its staff leaning sideways over a log. Next to the flagstaff a body lay face down.

Archer waved at a squad on one side of the body. "Not everybody. Second squad, you move fifty yards up this ridge and keep your eyes out."

Cleary knelt alongside the gray-clad body and turned it over. Blue eyes stared vacantly at the sky. He brushed dirt from the boy's cheek.

"God, he's young."

Martin sneered, "Yeah, so? He's a rebel, a fucking rebel. He'd a been happy to see us all dead."

"What's he gonna do, shoot us with his flag?"

"He'd cheer if his buddies did!"

"He ain't cheerin' nothin' now."

They stood in silence, looking down at the flag bearer. One leg of his uniform pants was shredded almost to the knee. His tunic, all its buttons gone, hung to the sides of his thin body. A bloodstain surrounded a hole in his shirt.

Archer shook his head. "Okay guys, we can't stand here all day, we gotta get to Savannah. And keep your eyes open, his outfit may be up ahead."

22

Cleary gestured at the body. "We just gonna leave him here, Lieutenant?"

"We don't have any choice, we got a job to do."

Martin sneered. "Yeah, Cleary, you wanna carry him to Savannah?"

Archer pulled a map from his tunic and unfolded it. "The map says this is Hutchinson Island. I'll mark his location and we'll report it to the quartermaster when we get to Savannah."

Martin sneered again, "They gonna bury a rebel? Let him rot!"

December 21, 1864

> Archer's company and the rest of XIV Corps reaches Savannah with no additional enemy contact. Before they arrive, the Confederate troops retreat across the river and Savannah mayor Richard Arnold surrenders the city to the Union. Savannah's parks and squares fill with the soldiers' tents and shanties, one built with wood scavenged from a house under construction for Confederate General Hugh Mercer.

The day after the company set up their tents in Monterey Square, Cleary came up to Archer.

"Lieutenant, did the quartermaster say anythin' about gettin' that dead kid down by the river?"

"No, they didn't. I did tell 'em, but they didn't sound like they were real interested in fetchin' a body outta the marsh."

Cleary sighed. "Y'know, it just don't seem right, leavin' him there for the vultures. It just don't seem right."

"I know what ya mean, Cleary. I'll go see the quartermaster again."

23

Early the next morning, a shovel in one hand, an ax in the other, Archer called through a tent door.

"Cleary, you in there?"

Cleary stuck his head out. "So Lieutenant, guess those tools mean the quartermaster wasn't interested?"

"You guess right. They're busy feedin' troops and the folks in Savannah. There's damn little food in this city, they're close to starvin'. You busy this mornin'?"

"I'll get my boots on."

"It shouldn't be so bad a walk without carryin' packs and guns."

They walked north out of the city over a bridge that crossed the river to Hutchinson Island. It took two hours for them to reach the spot on Archer's map that marked the body. They saw the flag still leaning against a log, but as they got closer, they saw the vultures clustered around the body.

Archer screamed, "Get the hell out of here you bastards!"

The vultures flapped into the sky. The body laid as they'd left it, but its eyes were gone and the mouth was torn into a bloody gash.

Archer leaned over the torn body. "Damn, they've ripped him all up."

Cleary bent alongside him. "He's so young. Let's see if we can find out who he is."

He went through the boy's pocket. His battered wallet held no money, but there was a military identification card. Cleary read the card.

"Edward P. Gaillard from Winnsboro, South Carolina. Fourteen years old."

"Fourteen. Damn."

Some of the vultures circled above. Three had perched in the tops of dead trees, watching the two soldiers.

Archer gestured toward a clear spot uphill from the body.

"Looks like the diggin' won't be too bad up there."

The dark earth was softened by rain. They took turns on the shovel, using the ax to cut through tree roots. A woodpecker cackled its strident call as they dug. It took less than an hour to make a hole three feet deep. They dragged the body to the grave and began to cover it.

Leaning on his shovel, Cleary asked Archer, "Do you think we should say somethin'? Don't seem right to just put him in and not say anything?"

"What should we say?"

They finished filling the grave, pressed the earth flat and mounded more dirt on the top. Archer cut a section of tree limb and drove it into the ground at the head of the grave. Two feet protruded. He split the top of the marker and stuck the boy's identification card into the split. They stood silently awhile, Archer frowning, finally nodding to himself.

"Well God, here's your boy. One of 'em, anyhow, guess you been gettin' a lot these days. This one's Edward Gaillard from Winnsboro. He died thinking he was doin' somethin' good, somethin' important. I hope he was thinkin' that, but he probly was just scared, scared of dyin'. His life was awful short, awful short. I 'spect he didn't get to do very much with it. Probly never even kissed a girl. But here he is. Amen."

"Amen."

Cleary retrieved the boy's flag and shoved it in the ground alongside the marker.

"Guess this don't really hurt anythin'."

A gentle wind fluttered the flag. A Carolina wren wheedled in the woods and crows cawed as the flock flew through the treetops.

Archer looked up at the crows.

"Y'know what they call a flock of crows, Cleary?"

"No."

"A murder."

They started back toward Savannah. Crossing the bridge onto the mainland, Cleary spoke.

"How much longer you think we're gonna be fightin', Lieutenant?"

"I think it's pretty much over, think the rebels know they're licked. God knows I hope it's over, I've sure as hell had enough of it, enough folks dyin', enough sloggin' through mud and rain and livin' in a damn tent. I used to love bein' outdoors but I've had enough of it to last the rest of my life. And enough shootin'! I don't think I'll ever go huntin' again."

"Yeah, I know what you mean. A gun means somethin' real different to me now than what it used to."

****

The army rested in Savannah a month, recuperating from wounds and illnesses. Archer visited four of his men, suffering intensely from dysentery in the hospital. Sherman focused on feeding the hungry citizens and the horde of Black refugees who'd followed his troops. As December approached its end, Archer called the company together under a sweeping live oak on the river bank.

"Congratulations to you all for doin' what you did on this campaign. We've got the rebels on the run, and we're gonna keep 'em that way."

A rumble agreement came from the men. "Yeah, lieutenant, they can't stand to us."

"We got a new year comin' up. I hope we don't get any real action, but you never know. We've got a good bit to celebrate when New Year's day hits, but don't be celebratin' too hard."

Private Martin spoke up. "Ah, c'mon lieutenant, it's time for some fun! There's plenny a whiskey in this town needs drinkin' and we've had damn little chance to do that lately."

"Yeah, I know, but remember this damn war's not over. We've got a chance to rest up awhile here, get our strength back, and I don't want you spendin' your time drunk and gettin' in fights. Go ahead and celebrate the New Year, we sure got reason to celebrate, but don't get crazy.

"General Sherman's keepin' a close eye on us. He sent down orders, they're posted at headquarters, 'bout how we're supposed to act and how we're not supposed to act. Basically, they say we gotta be on good behavior. Don't get drunk and don't take stuff that don't belong to you. Don't cuss at the locals."

"Can I cuss quiet?"

"If you can cuss quiet enough they can't hear you, I guess. But be aware he ain't kiddin' around. The orders say anybody actin' unsoldierly will be shot."

Martin raised his hand. "Is it okay if we talk to the girls? They sure got some pretty girls down here."

"Yeah, you can talk to them, but from what I see and hear, they won't be doin' much talkin' back at you. They ain't real fond of us."

Cleary spoke, "Any idea where we'll be headin' from here?"

"I haven't been told, but I'd guess we'll head up into South Carolina, maybe Charleston. There's not much left to the south."

February 15, 1865

When they leave Savannah, the XIV Corps doesn't go to Charleston, but to Columbia, South Carolina's capital. As the two-mile troop column approaches the city on the curving state road by the Broad River, General Sherman rides the column's length. Now remounted on his gelding Goldie, Archer salutes from the saddle as the general rides past. His men wave and hurrah at the man they call Uncle Billy.

27

Sherman, in his chronically rumpled
uniform, waves back.

The stone bridge over the Broad River had been destroyed during the
war. Its stones lay on the river bed, water flowing over and around
them. Homes and farms, some large, some small, many apparently
abandoned, bordered the road. Some showed damage from the
fighting, porch roofs hanging askew, walls riddled with bullet holes.
Women and children peered through doors and windows at the
passing troops. Cotton fluff stuck in the weeds, hung on the shrubs in
the yards, on the plants in the gardens.

It's said that an army fights on its stomach, and the stomachs of
Sherman's troops were filled almost entirely with supplies foraged
from Confederate homes and farms. The bummers assigned foraging
duty were far less disciplined than the regular troops. In addition to
the empty pantries and hog pens in their wake lay burned homes and
businesses.

Between the bummers and the regular troops, little was left.
Where troops had stopped to feed their horses, folks gathered the
kernels of corn the horses dropped, parched them and ate them. They
parched and ate acorns. Salt was impossible to get. Some dug up the
salty earth under their smokehouses, soaked it in water and used the
water to salt their food.

February 16, 1865

The five-hundred-pound bales stacked
in Columbia's streets, smoldering when
the XIV Corps arrived, are blazing. A
pall of smoke hangs over the city.
Sherman's troops work to extinguish the
fire, the general himself working
alongside them. Their initial efforts

28

appear successful, but the next day violent winds lash the smoldering bales and the fire flares again. Wind-driven balls of cotton land on roofs and in yards, the flames leap from building to building, entire blocks of homes and businesses blaze.

The fire wasn't totally subdued until Saturday, February 18. By that time, 80 of the city's 124 blocks were devastated. That day, Columbia Mayor Thomas Goodwyn surrendered the city to the Federals as the last of the Confederate troops escaped, burning the bridge over the Congaree behind them.

Jubilant Union soldiers found the city's liquor stores and celebrated their victory enthusiastically, many getting thoroughly drunk. The chaos was compounded by looting, drunken soldiers and civilians storming into houses, stealing food and valuables. Army command issued orders to restore order but, with many soldiers participating in the lawlessness, it didn't come quickly. Frank was able to assemble little more than half his company; the remainder— including Private Martin—were not there as he passed the orders on.

Carolyn

February 24, 1865

Winnsboro

Heading north from Columbia, Frank's company reaches Winnsboro's southern edge early in the morning. The bummers had entered the town several days previously and treated it in typical bummer manner, setting twenty of Winnsboro's buildings, including the

29

Episcopal church, afire. Smoke still rises from ruined buildings.

The Fluker farmhouse on the west side of the road is essentially undamaged. As the company approaches it, Carolyn is sweeping cotton fluff from the front porch. Carolyn has been enslaved on the Fluker's 200-acre farm since birth. Cholera took her mother when she was five. The next year it took her father, Herbert Ringgold. A white man, he'd owned a farm three miles from the Flukers.

Sixteen years old, Carolyn has become a true beauty. Sparkling green eyes shine from her brown face. Her body is fully a woman's, curves insisting through her homespun dress. Her entire life's been spent on the Fluker farm and she's become much more than a house slave to Elinor Fluker. Despite state law making it illegal, like many slave owners, Elinor Fluker taught her to read and write and do arithmetic. And she loves to read.

Elinor's husband and all six of her sons served in the Confederate army. Of the seven, six are dead. Only Robert is still alive.

Carolyn and Elinor are the only people in the big house since the army took Robert. As the house grows quieter

30

and quieter and the bad news cascades,
Elinor withdraws into herself. Much of
Carolyn's energy is now spent on simply
encouraging her to get out of bed, get
dressed, do something—anything—
other than lament.

She was leaning on her broom as Archer's company
approached. He reined his horse from the column and turned into the
Fluker front yard, dismounted and tipped his hat to her.

"Excuse me, miss, but do you have any water? My horse is dry
as can be. And I could sure use some myself."

She was surprised at the man's politeness. Miz Fluker had
painted Yankee soldiers as rude, not to be trusted. She went to the side
of the house, filled the bucket hanging from the well's crossbeam and
set it in the front yard without speaking.

Archer held Goldie away from the bucket. "Do you have a cup
handy? I'd like to grab a drink before Goldie slobbers in the pail."

She fetched a cup from the house.

"Thank you."

As Archer drank, Carolyn noticed his wound. Two fingers
were gone from his left hand. Red scar tissue stretched from the back
of the hand to its palm. But that didn't hurt his looks. He was tall,
brown hair long but combed. His face was craggy, dominated by his
nose. And nice blue eyes.

He filled the cup and drank several times. "OK boy, your turn
now."

Goldie jammed his muzzle into the bucket and slurped
greedily. Stepping forward, he hit the bucket with a front foot and it
tipped over.

"Oops, I'm sorry, he's so thirsty he's forgot his manners. Could
you get a little more?"

Carolyn refilled the bucket. "He sure is thirsty. You been

31

riding far?"

"You might say that. We started in Atlanta and ended up in Savannah. Before that we were in Tennessee." Archer couldn't keep his eyes off the girl. Just as steadily she watched him, her eyes shining from her brown face. So beautiful, a bright sparkling green.

"How much further you goin?"

"Right now we're just lookin' for a place to camp for the night. After that, well, I'm not supposed to say, but I think we're heading north."

He raised his hat and nodded. "I sure thank you for the water, and Goldie does too." He swung into the saddle, looked back and tipped his hat again.

Yes, she's a negro. But my god, so beautiful. And those eyes!

The next evening he rode into the Fluker's yard again, a private behind him. Carolyn came to the door. He removed his hat and nodded at the soldier.

"This is Private Johnson. Things are gettin' pretty rough in some parts of town, and he's gonna keep an eye on your house till it calms down."

"Is that really necessary? Nothin' bad's happened here."

"Well, that's not true everywhere. I'd feel a lot better if you had some kind of protection. I'll come back soon as I can, but in the meantime, his duty's at your house. If that's okay with you."

"Jes' a minute, I'll check with Miz Fluker."

She called through the door. Elinor Fluker, sixty, gray hair crushed in a bun behind her head, face deeply lined, came onto the porch. Archer repeated what he'd told Carolyn. She frowned at Archer and Johnson, a lanky boy with a mop of hair hanging from the back of his cap. He shuffled his feet and shifted his Spencer carbine from one shoulder to the other.

"Alright." She went back in the house.

Archer mounted Goldie and tipped his hat. "Johnson, you know your job. Keep these folks safe."

Carolyn watched as Archer rode away in the direction of Columbia.

> *Sure is good of him to put this boy here*
> *to keep an eye on us, they's no way he*
> *can be doin' this for everybody in*
> *Winnsboro. Mebbe it's me, he sure been*
> *talkin' nice. And lookin' nice too.*
> *Wonder where he's from? Mebbe he's*
> *got a woman back there*

Archer returned two days later. As he looped Goldie's reins over the porch railing, Carolyn was again sweeping the porch, her broom now pushing ashes. They covered the porch, the roof, the lawn, hung on the bushes. She filled the water pail and brought it to the horse. Private Johnson sat on the porch steps, Carolyn on the porch swing.

Frank gestured at the swing, "Is is okay if I sit there?"

"Yes."

"There's some good news, my company's been assigned to provost duty in the city. We won't be heading north with the rest of the army, we'll be stayin' here awhile." He nodded at Johnson. "How's it been at the house, has Johnson here been doin' his job?"

"Well yes, he's been doin' jes fine, and we were mighty glad to have him."

He turned to Johnson."Did somethin' happen?"

"Well sir, there was a bit of trouble. Some rowdy troops came to the house, said they were lookin' for food, but I don't know that was the truth. I mean, I'm sure the troops get enough to eat from the army mess. These rowdies were already liquored up, they were lookin' for more drink and whatever else they could grab." He glanced at Carolyn. "But they weren't too hard to discourage." He moved his Spencer slightly.

"Thank you, Johnson, you obviously did a good job. Has Miz Carolyn been able to find you somethin' to eat?"

33

"Yes, sir, she has, bread and hominy mostly. When she cooks up bacon, that too."

"You stayin' warm enough?"

"Yessir, when it gets cold nights, there's a pretty warm shed around the side."

"That's good, Johnson, keep up the good work."

"Thank you, sir."

Frank stood up, looked at Carolyn. "I'll come by tomorrow, see how things are goin'."

"That'd be nice, Mister Archer."

"If it's okay with you, you could just call me Frank."

"It's okay. I'm Carolyn."

Carolyn watched as he mounted his horse and rode away. Despite her beauty, romance hadn't been part of her life. The Flukers hadn't encouraged it, and her contact with men her age had been limited. Some had smiled at her in the grocery store and from the balcony at the church, but she'd always been with Miz Fluker.

She was only twelve when the war broke out and now, many men were gone. Blacks had left Winnsboro in droves, some following the Union army and being grouped in army-organized camps. Many of the white ones were dead.

The feelings she had as she watched him go were very new. He was white, yes, but those feelings were very real.

Frank did come by the next evening. He started up the porch steps and, not by chance, Carolyn opened the front door before he could knock.

Again they sat on the swing.

"How long have you lived here, Carolyn?

"Been her all my life. My momma was a slave for Miz Fluker, but she died when I's just a little girl. Never knew my daddy at all."

"So you were a slave for the Flukers?"

"Yeah, but they didn't hardly treat me like a slave. Miz Fluker, she's been more like a momma to me. Taught me to read 'n write 'n everythin'."

"You like to read?"

"Oh yeah, read 'bout everythin' I gets my hands on. Just read 'Alice in Wonderland' by Charles Dickens, didn't unnerstan' it all, but it was a lot of fun."

"You think I should read it?"

"I think you'd like it, think mos' everybody would like it. And Miz Fluker, she's got a big shelf fulla books, I'm sure she'd let you borrow some."

****

For the rest of that month and part of the next, Archer's company provided security in Columbia. They arrested looters and drunks and watched the city's citizens, mostly women and children, claw through the blackened remnants of their homes, retrieving cookware, jewelry, treasured mementos. With resentful order returned to the city, he relieved Johnson of his post.

Frank spent almost every evening on the Fluker porch with Carolyn, and that didn't escape Elinor Fluker's attention. One morning as the two of them shared a breakfast of grits, she confronted Carolyn.

"That Yankee sure's been payin' you attention. What's goin' on?"

"Well, he likes me, he's makin' that clear."

"And you?"

"Yeah, I like him too. He's a real nice man, polite and respectful and all."

"But he's a Yankee, his durn army's wrecked our town, our state. And they killed 'most all my men, I hate them!"

"I know, I know, and he hates it too. He hates the war, hates all the destruction. He's not here 'cause he chose it, he got drafted just like our boys did. And he's hurtin' too. His best friend Samuel, they got drafted together, he was killed at Chattanooga, same time Frank got his hand shot."

"I know you're gettin' to be a woman now, and maybe it is time you found yourself a man, but why this man?"

Carolyn frowned, stared at her grits. "Well, he is a good man. And you know, there just ain't many men around here any more. Probly half the colored men done run off, followin' the Federal army when it come through, and a whole lot of our men either been killed or they's lyin' in a bed somewhere with a piece of 'em shot off. They just ain't hardly no men left."

"But he's White. You know the two a you's walkin' on shaky ground gettin' involved like this. Lotta folks around here ain't gonna like it."

"I know, I know. But what can I do?"

"Look girl, I know what you're sayin'. But you know what, I know you know this, I love you, doan' care if you are colored. I just doan' want you to get hurt."

When Frank arrived at the Fluker's a week later, Carolyn had horrible news. Robert, Elinor's only surviving son, has been killed in a skirmish with Sherman's troops near Cheraw. His body lies in an Army mortuary in Columbia.

"Miz Fluker's jes' crushed, hasn't eat a thing since she heard, jes' lies in her bed, won't hardly talk."

"Oh god, I'm so sorry. You can't get her to eat?"

"No. Sometimes she'll drink a little water, that's all. The army folks, they said we should come get Robert if we wanna bury him, otherwise they'll do it somewhere."

"We can bury him."

That afternoon, using boards salvaged from a decrepit shed, Johnson and Archer built a rough casket, carried it by wagon to the mortuary and returned with Robert's body. It sat in the Fluker living room, Elinor beside it, until noon the next day. The men loaded the casket in the wagon and Elinor sat sobbing on it, a black veil over her face, Carolyn beside her. Johnson slapped the haunch of the borrowed

36

mule hitched to the wagon and it lurched forward. Archer rode alongside.

The day was bitter cold, gray. The wagon's steel-rimmed wheels rattled over the road, rutted by the passage of Sherman's cannon and wagons and layered with ash. Gray ash lay on crushed shrubs and flowers, houses, everywhere. Yard fences leaned drunkenly, some flattened when the Union troops had passed. A belly-bloated horse covered with flies lay in the front yard of a burned house. The air stank of ash and death. Except for Elinor's sobbing, the group was silent for the half-hour trip to the graveyard.

Behind the Convent Baptist Church, fresh earth was heaped alongside the hole Johnson and Archer had dug next to Robert's father's gravestone.

Pierce Fluker
Sharpsburg Maryland
September 17, 1862

Of Elinor's family, these two graves were the only ones she would know. The bodies of the five other boys probably lay in mass graves at Manassas and Shiloh. Or lay rotting in woods where they'd fallen. Remnants of soldiers' bodies were found for years after the war's conclusion.

All seven of these men had fought for the Confederacy, but some families, both North and South, weren't so uniform in dedication. One Savannah family's six sons were evenly split, three fighting for the Federals, three for the Confederacy. Three sons sworn to kill the other three.

Sweating, the men slid the coffin from the wagon onto the ground, laying it on two ropes spread across the hole. Reverend Collington said the funeral words, then apologized.

"I'm sorry we don't have the manpower to do this proper, my friends, but right now we just don't. This war has changed a lot of things. The niggers who used to do this have left, gone off with the Yankees. We're gonna have to put Robert's coffin in ourselves."

They pulled the ropes—Carolyn and Archer on one, Johnson and the preacher on the other—until the coffin hung above the grave. It tipped, one edge scraped earth from the hole's side.

Archer said, "Carolyn, can you hold it?"

"Yes, I got it." She struggled with the rope but held it. The coffin straightened as it descended, lid now facing the sullen sky, the ropes cutting grooves in the grave's sides. Dirt sprinkled onto the pine lid, gradually stopped when when the coffin reached the bottom of the hole. Carolyn dropped her rope, looked at her hands as she stretched them.

Archer said, "Are you okay, are your hands okay?"

"Yeah, I'm fine."

Archer and Johnson pulled the ropes from under the coffin and dropped them by the side of the grave. "Okay, let's take them home, Johnson. We'll cover the grave later."

Elinor Fluker had cried silently through the entire service and was still crying as Archer took her arm and helped her into the wagon. Carolyn, tears glistening on her cheeks, sat next to her, an arm over her shoulder. Johnson turned the mule and the wagon started home.

Elinor stayed in her bed for two days after the funeral, silent. Early the third day, Carolyn urged her out of bed and helped her dress. She cooked, put food in front of her, but Elinor ate little. She sat in the parlor, staring blankly. When her eyes did focus, it was on the photos on the mantel. Her sons and her husband.

April 1865

Compared to marching and fighting, security duty has been a blessing. With his days largely predictable, Archer's spent almost every evening since

February with Carolyn. Their
differences are big, but the more time
they spend together, the less those
differences seem to matter. In fact, they
add to their growing attraction.

He told her about growing up in Buckeystown, and no, he didn't have
a girl back there waiting for him. About getting drafted and moving
with the army. How sickened he was of the war, of seeing people
wounded, killed. About Samuel's death. How he lost his fingers.

As they sat on the porch one warm April evening, she told him
some of what life was like being enslaved.

"Well, when you're little, it's just the way it is, it's the way it's
always been and feels like always will be. My mama, all the old
people, they was slaves ever since they was born, they daddies and
mamas was and they daddies and mamas too. The white people, they
tell you what to do, and you get hit or whipped if'n you doan' do it.

""Course as you grow up you realize they's just people too, and
it's jes' like an accident that they get to be the bosses. You realize God
didn't set down some rule that makes white skin a better person than
black skin. And some 'a the stuff that happens, it just don't feel right,
just not how one human person should act to another one. They's a
whole lot of those things, some of 'em's big, some of 'em's little. But
they happen to you, or you hear about 'em, most every day.

"They's a big farm northa town, the Lemon Plantation. I got to
know one of the slave gals from there, name's Annie, when they come
into town to get food and farm stuff. Her mama was a wet nurse, she
nursed the white babies—think they was three of 'em—that the
plantation lady had. That white lady, maybe she didn't have 'nuff milk,
maybe she just didn't wanna sit around nursin' a baby.

"Well, Annie's mama, after awhile she stopped makin' milk.
Maybe she got too old, maybe somethin' else happened, I dunno. With
no milk, she waren't no use no more to the white folks, so they sold

39

her. Sold the woman nursed three of their children. Jes' like you'd sell a cow that quit givin' milk.

"'Course they doan' need that kinda excuse, not any excuse, to sell a slave. Lots of the folks I know, their mama or their kids or husband been sold just cause the owner needed money. Sommathem owners doan' think nothin' bout breakin' up a family like that."

Frank shook his head. "Must be damn hard living all the time knowin' most of the white folks look at you and see somethin' kin to a cow."

"Well yes, but 'most all colored folks know them white folk's heads is messed up, even if they's the ones givin' the orders. And they not all like that. Mister and Miz Fluker, they never was. Miz Fluker, she's been a lot like a mama to me. She never treated me like no cow."

"Cow's the last thing comes to my mind when I look at you. You're 'bout the most beautiful woman I've ever seen."

Two days later, Archer returned late in the afternoon. He kicked his legs out of the stirrups, leaned forward on Goldie's neck, slid slowly off the horse. He was bareheaded, his uniform pants and shirt soaked with sweat and stained with blood. He sat on the porch steps.

Carolyn came out on the porch. Her face dropped. "You look awful. Are you hurt?"

"No, I'm okay, none of this blood's from me. My company's been helping out at the hospitals in the city. 'Course, they're not really hospitals, they're just houses big enough to have a table or two where the surgeons do what they can for the wounded. The floors are covered in blood."

Hand over her mouth, Carolyn shook her head.

"It's just awful, guys screamin' and groanin'. Guys are dyin' all the time. Some of our work was carryin' buckets and wheelbarrows filled with arms and legs out of the houses, diggin' holes and buryin' them."

"Oh god. How horrible."

40

Elbows on knees, he leaned forward and buried his face in his hands. "I'll never forget it."

Carolyn stroked his hair. "I'll get you some of Miz Fluker's husband's clothes. Come in the house, take those things off and I'll try to get the blood out of 'em. There's a screen over in the corner of the dinin' room, slide a chair in there and give me your clothes."

Frank undressed behind the screen and handed his clothes out. Carolyn brought him pants and a shirt and they went out on the porch.

"Thanks for doin' those clothes. I hope the blood comes out."

"I think it will, I've got 'em soakin' now. Do you need 'em back soon?"

"No, not really. We're not supposed to be outta uniform, but now that the war's over the men, even the officers, ain't payin' strict attention to the rules. It'd be nice if you could do 'em in a coupla days."

"Think I can do that."

He stretched his arms out. Pierce Fluker's shirt was a bit too small, his wrists stuck out of the sleeves.

"I do feel a lot better outta those bloody clothes."

"I can tell you do."

"Y'know what, I've got the mornin' off tomorrow. How'd you like to spend it together? We'll take Goldie for a ride."

"That does sound nice. Should be nice'n cool in the mornin'. I only been on a horse oncet before, and that waren't really a horse, was a mule."

He stood, held out a hand to her. "So it's a date?"

She stood, took his hand. "It's a date. See you in the mornin'."

Shortly after sunrise, Carolyn sat on the front porch. A gentle breeze out of the west drifted the smell of something fresh cut—early hay?—to her. Across the road a fox poked through the undergrowth, sticking its nose hard into the grass and weeds. A mouse scurried from one clump, the fox clamped a paw on it, tossed it in the air with its mouth,

41

grabbed it, tossed it again.

He mus' not be very hungry, playin' with his breakfast. Poor mouse.

In the branches of scrub oaks lining the road, vultures had awakened, spread their wings facing the sun, drying the night's dew from their feathers. From the direction of the just-risen sun, a hawk screamed.

She heard the sound of hooves on the road. Then, there he was, Frank on Goldie.

I never felt 'bout a man like this before. Guess I'm fallin' in love. Yes, do believe I'm fallin' in love.

As he rode into the yard, she stood up.

"Well, look at you! I didn't know you wore pants."

"This be the firs' time I ever did, far as I 'member. Las' time I went ridin' I had to ride sideways 'cause of my skirt, and I didn't like that none. These pants was Pierce Junior's, he was right skinny, all I had to do was fold the legs up a bit. Whaddya think?"

He looked her up and down, frowned, nodded his head.

"I dunno that they're gonna replace skirts all the time, but I think they're a good idea for today. Turn around."

She turned slowly, bending her neck to face him, raising her eyebrows, questioning with her eyes as she finished the circle.

"Well, yes ma'am, they are pants, but ain't nobody gonna think you're a boy."

She giggled.

"Okay, you're all dressed, git on over here and git on this horse."

He took his right foot out of the stirrup, held it sideways with his foot, reached both arms down under her shoulders.

"Stick your right foot in the stirrup."

As he lifted her to place her foot, he felt his hands touch the sides of her breasts. She felt them too.

"Good, now swing your left leg over his neck."

She slid into place on the saddle in front of him.

"What's this lump under me?"

"That's the pommel, here, I can make a little more room for you."

He slid back on the saddle.

"Ah, that's better. Now they's room."

They rode down Main Street and turned east toward the woods. Sometimes he rode with both hands on the reins. When they crossed a ditch or mounted a rise he clasped one arm around her waist. She leaned back into him.

"Y'know, riding this way feels a whole lot different than riding sideways. Feels a lot steadier, a lot more solid."

"Yes, that sidesaddle stuff is really silly. It's a good way to fall off."

What Carolyn didn't tell Frank was how good she felt. They'd never been this close, never touched like this. Most of the time her back was against him and his arm was around her waist. And the pommel felt good under her. As Goldie lunged to mount a rise or step off one, the saddle massaged her crotch gently.

Winnsboro was quickly left behind. They rode a trail through scattered woods to a creek.

"I've walked here a coupla times," she said, "this's McCulley Creek."

The creek flowed south clean and clear. Frank slid her off Goldie, tied him to a tree and pulled a blanket from the saddlebag.

"Came all prepared, didn't ya?"

"We don't wanna get those nice pants of yours all dirty, do we?" He spread the blanket on the bank of the creek.

"I didn't think to bring anything to eat," she said, "I coulda made some sandwiches or somethin'."

"That's okay. I've got everythin' I need just bein' with you."

A big bird with white and blue feathers glided over the creek, extended its legs and splashed into the edge of the creek twenty yards

43

downstream.

"That's a great blue heron," he said, "We've got 'em up in Buckeystown, didn't know you had 'em down here."

"Yeah, you see 'em a lot anywhere there's water."

They watched the heron stalk slowly through the creek shallows. It stepped deliberately, then froze, staring into the water. The curve in its long neck uncurled explosively, lancing the pointed beak down. A fish flapped on its point when it rose. The bird flipped the fish up in the air and caught it as it fell.

"Looks like he's got breakfast."

They sat in silence, watching the heron stalk the creek. It speared two more fish.

"Carolyn?"

"Mmmm?"

"Can I kiss you?"

She turned to him, green eyes shining from her brown face.

"Yes. Yes."

They kissed.

"Do you know I'm falling in love with you?"

"Yes."

"Do you feel the same way?"

She nodded slowly.

"Yes."

"Will you marry me?"

"Yes."

They kissed again, a long, slow kiss, then sat in silence, eyes worshiping each other.

Frank broke the quiet.

"Do you think we can make a home here? I mean, you bein' colored and me bein' white, how much trouble you think folks here gonna give us?"

"It ain't gonna be easy. They's a few couples like that, but mostly they stay outta sight."

44

"If it can't work here we can go up to Maryland, folks ain't so bad there. They ain't perfect, but they ain't so bad. Would you go up there with me, I mean if we had to?"

Carolyn sat in silence.

Could I leave the farm, the only home I've ever known? Could I leave Miz Fluker? Well, that's something I'd have to deal with. But I'd be leaving with Frank, he'd be my husband then and I'd be his wife.

"Yes." They sat on the blanket holding hands for another hour. The heron speared more fish.

She leaned back into him as they rode home, his arm tight around her.

April 9, 1865

> General Lee surrenders to Grant at Appomattox and the war essentially comes to an end, though—since Lee's Army of Northern Virginia is only one of the three Confederate armies— sporadic fighting continues. Told of the surrender, General Wade Hampton of the Army of the Tennessee gathers his men and tells them it is "a rumor I do not believe." Not until Union soldiers capture Jefferson Davis on May 10 does he abandon that belief.

That evening Frank, Carolyn and Elinor sat at the supper table, eating grits and bean soup.

Carolyn held up Elinor's spoon, "Miz Fluker, you try some of this soup now, it's good and you need it. You gotta keep your strength up."

Elinor took two sips of soup, set her spoon down. "Why? Keep my strength up for what? For what?"

Frank set his spoon down. "I'll tell you for what. So you can give your blessing to me and Carolyn getting married. And so you can come to our wedding."

Despite Elinor having talked with Carolyn and seeing them together all those evenings on the porch, she was still surprised. "Wedding? You're gonna get married?"

"Yes."

"You don't care that she's colored?"

"No ma'am, I don't."

"Carolyn, how d'you feel about this?"

"Well, I really didn't imagine it could happen, but it did. I love him and he loves me."

Elinor was quiet for a minute. She looked hard at Frank, frowned, then at Carolyn. "Y'know, if you plan to live down here, it ain't gonna be easy."

Carolyn nodded. "I know, but some folks do it."

"When're you gonna get married?"

Frank smiled. "We didn't set a date yet, we were kind of waiting for this war to be completely over. And we wanted to ask you."

"You didn't need to ask me. Yes, I know I own her, at least I used to, but I never really wanted to. She owns herself."

At the end of the meal, as Carolyn cleared bowls from the table, Elinor gestured to Frank.

"Come with me."

Frank followed as she walked haltingly up the stairs to her bedroom. She opened a dresser drawer and took out a ring.

"You'd have an awful time finding a ring around here, given how destroyed this town is. I want you to have this, for Carolyn."

"Miz Fluker, I don't know, I mean that's part of your family."

"What family? Yes, it was part of my family, it was mine and

46

my mother's. But she's gone, has been for twenty years. And what other family? Pierce? My sons? Thanks to this war, they're all gone, there'll be no wives' fingers they could put it on! What do I have left, what other than Carolyn? Who else would it mean something to?"

She held the plain gold band out to Frank.

"I don't know what to say. I just can't thank you enough. But thank you. Thank you."

The next day, Archer stopped at Convent Baptist Church and talked to Reverend Collington.

"Marry you and that nigger gal? I don't do that. No sir, I can't do that. No sir!"

Archer turned on his heel. What were they going to do? Travel all the way to Maryland or somewhere farther north where the churches and preachers didn't look at a colored skin and see somebody not really human?

He and Carolyn talked about it that evening.

"Well, of course he won't marry us. You gettin' a tiny taste of what colored folks been dealin' with every day of our lives."

"Well it stinks."

"We could jump the broom if you want." She explained what enslaved people often did to mark their commitment in marriage, jumping over a broomstick in a ceremony.

"That sounds like fun, but I'm used to folks gettin' married by a preacher. Mebbe later we could do a broom."

An idea struck him. A chaplain could marry folks.

The next day he met with the chaplain of the Army of the Cumberland and explained the problem. Father Joseph Carrier was Catholic, but during the war, neither the chaplains nor the troops paid strict attention to their nominal religions. God's rules got simplified if you were dying or a soldier you held was dying. The joy and hope of a wedding was a wonderful change from the chaplain's daily rituals of death.

Four days later, Archer commandeered a buggy. Drawn by the same borrowed mule that had pulled the wagon with Robert Fluker's body, it carried Elinor and Carolyn to the army tent where Father Carrier held daily services. Private Johnson drove the mule, Archer rode behind.

Some of the remnants of Columbia's fires and fighting were gone by then. Wind and rain had cleaned ash from the land and the trees. The carcasses of dead livestock had been buried.

The little group and some of Archer's army company clustered in front of the tent's altar. His eyes locked on Carolyn for the entire brief ceremony. Her eyes were not as bold as his, but as he slipped Elinor's mother's ring on her finger she raised them.

So green, so beautiful.

Archer's smile stretched his face. "I will love you as long as love can last. My heart says it will be forever."

"Mine does too."

Returning home after the wedding, the little group stopped at the graveyard behind Convent Baptist Church. Elinor Fluker sat in the buggy in silence. Reverend Collington frowned from a window at the back of the church as Archer and Johnson took a carved oak marker from the buggy, shoveled a slit at the head of Robert Fluker's grave and rocked the marker in place.

Robert Fluker
Died February 18, 1865
for the Honor of the South.

April 16, 1865

> Early this morning, the commanding colonel assembles all the provost troops at brigade headquarters in Columbia.

48

Archer and the other lieutenants are called into his office where he reads a telegram from Secretary of War Edwin Stanton.

***Abraham Lincoln died this morning at 22 minutes after* seven**

The officers are stunned.

The colonel continues. "The army has directed that all communities under our supervision will recognize this for what it is, a tragedy. Every home in Columbia and the surrounding towns are to display black on the front of their house. Lincoln was president of this entire country, including the damn rebels, and they will recognize that.

"I want your men to go every house, tell the residents what's happened and that they are to display a piece of black cloth, black anything, on their houses. They will recognize this tragedy for what it is. Anybody who doesn't will spend time in the stockade. You are dismissed."

Archer leaves the office shaking his head.

What a task! Tell all these folks to put black on their homes to honor a man most of them hate, blame for everything that's happened, everything they's lost. Or go to jail.

He gathered his men and told them of Lincoln's murder. They were dismayed, then furious.

"They don't know who did it? Had to be some rebel bastard!"

"We oughta string the whole damn state up, burn everything in it!"

Archer raised his hands. "Hold up, now. We're all angry, yeah, but let's remember, the folks here didn't do it, they didn't kill the president. Mostly what's left here are women and children, not fighters, and they're already paying a pretty awful price. Their homes, their families, their farms. And some of them were against the war from the beginning."

"Yeah, and we're not paying that price?"

"Yes, we are paying an awful price, for sure. But beatin' up on civilians won't change that. And the army won't stand for it. I won't stand for it."

He unrolled a map of Columbia. "We're dividing the city up into blocks. Sergeant O'Shaugnessy will split you into teams, each team will have a piece, four or five city blocks. You're to knock on every door and tell them they must put black on the front of their houses to recognize the president's death. Black cloth, black crepe, black whatever.

"If they refuse they'll be put in the stockade. But no other threats, understand? No violence, no insults. Just tell them. And tomorrow we'll patrol the city again to make sure they complied."

He spread the map on the back of a wagon. "Now c'mon up and the sergeant will give you your assignments."

As his men gathered around the map he called Private Johnson over to one side.

"You and I are gonna take Winnsboro."

Johnson and Archer pastured their horses behind the Fluker home and walked to the town's north end. Like many of the homes, the last house in town was dilapidated, paint flaking from the walls, boards missing from the porch floor. Archer knocked on the door.

50

A woman opened it, her face creased and tired, a frown of disgust on her mouth. Two young children peeked around the edge of her tattered skirt. Archer figured she wasn't very old, for there was no gray in the hair pinned atop her head or the strands that escaped and hung on a cheek. Probably widowed.

She stared at him without speaking.

"Ma'am, I've been ordered to pass news to you. It's been reported President Lincoln was shot and is dead. To recognize his passing, all homes are ordered to display black on the front of the house."

Her mouth twitched, she looked down, then back at him. She said nothing.

"Ma'am, this is an order from the government. You must display black on your house."

"If I don't?"

"You'll be put in jail."

She nodded slowly. "Mmmm. Black. Guess that fits, don't it?"

"Fits?"

"Yeah, it fits." She closed the door slowly.

By Saturday, black cloth hung on every house in Winnsboro and Columbia, including those on the roads in and out of the city. But not from the Fluker's. Archer had left her to the last. He and Carolyn sat in the front room with Elinor trying to convince her.

Carolyn leaned toward Elinor, "It's jes' a piece a cloth, ma'am, jes' a piece a cloth!"

"I will not recognize that man's death! This war was his fault, it's all his fault, he should spend eternity in hell!"

Archer shook his head. "Miz Fluker, you've simply got to. The army'll put you in jail if you don't."

"I won't!"

"Ma'am, I understand how you feel, I do, but there isn't any choice. How about if I put up the cloth?"

She grimaced, stood up from the couch and walked up the stairs. Her bedroom door slammed.

They sat silently for a minute.

"Think that means yes, Carolyn?"

"Well, it weren't a no. Go ahead and do it. Sure don't want her goin' to jail."

That evening, Carolyn took a meager supper up to Elinor's room. Elinor lay in bed.

"Here's some supper, Miz Fluker, just some soup and grits. It's all we got right now, but Frank's gonna take me to the army commissary tomorrow, we'll get some meat. They've got all sortsa food."

Elinor nodded slowly. "That's good."

"You eat that up now, you'll feel better."

"Thank you, dear girl. I will."

****

As Frank and Carolyn leave for the commissary the next morning, black cloth hangs from the decorative molding above the Fluker porch. From her bed, Elinor hears them leave. She dresses, walks slowly down the stairs and out to the shed, where she cuts a length of rope. She carries the rope back in the house and out to the front porch, dragging a kitchen chair behind her. She puts the chair at the edge of the porch, climbs onto it, pulls down the black cloth and throws it on the ground.

The day was warm with a gentle breeze from the west. A gust blew the cloth over the flower bed to an azalea, where it stuck fluttering. Elinor got off the chair, ripped it from the azalea's branches and threw it in the dirt. She crushed it into the earth with a heel, climbed back on the chair and knotted the rope around her neck with a crude sliding knot. She looped the loose end over the molding and tied it.

She stood on the chair a long time. Nobody came past the house.

And what do I have now.
Nothing.

She kicked the back of the chair. It tipped, fell from beneath her and clattered down the porch steps. The rope ended her fall with a jerk. One shoe fell off, followed the chair down the steps. Her legs kicked, her hands clutched at the strangling noose as it crushed her neck. Her body spasmed, then swung slowly, the toes of its left foot brushing a shred of cotton on the porch.

The next day the mule cart again rattled over the dirt road to Convent Baptist Church. After a brief funeral service, Elinor Fluker was laid to rest beside her husband and Robert.

Elinor Fluker
Loving wife and mother
Taken by the War
April 17, 1865

Given the Proclamation, it was unnecessary, but Elinor's will included language freeing Carolyn, stating that she'd "given her time," the words traditionally used to free slaves. It also left Carolyn the house and farm.

A week after the burial, Carolyn was straightening up Elinor's room, stripping the bed, organizing her personal affects. She called to Frank downstairs.

"Frank, come up here a minute."

She'd opened a lower drawer in Elinor's wardrobe. In the drawer were seven bundles of money, each tied with a wool thread and labeled with a name.

Pierce   **Robert**   **Pierce Jr**   **Arnold**   **Hugh**
               Terence   **Arthur**

"This is their army pay, she been keepin' it for when they come home."

Frank stared at the bundles of worthless Confederate bills. "Oh god. What should we do with it?"

"I dunno. It won't buy nothin'.

She slid the drawer closed. "I'll jes' put it back for now."

May 12, 1865

> Discharged from the army, Frank is alone on the porch one gray morning when a gaunt man comes up the walk wearing the gray pants of a Confederate uniform. Archer's seen him before, coming and going from a farm down the road. The right arm of his shirt is empty, rolled up and pinned at the shoulder.

He spoke. "Been seein' you here some. Guess you're a new neighbor?"

"You could say that. Looks like you've done some rough times."

"Yeah, you could say that too. Fightin' a war ain't what you call a picnic, and it sure ain't when you lose it."

"I'm sorry. I know they say we won, but it waren't any picnic this side either. What's your name?"

"Joshua. They call me Josh. You can call me Josh."

"I'm Frank. Good to make your acquaintance, Josh. Glad we're doin' it not pointin' guns at each other."

"Yeah. I see you took up with that nigger gal lives here."

"She's not a nigger, she's Carolyn, she's my wife."

"Oh. Well, I didn't mean nothin'. Congratulations, I guess. She's right purty."

"Yeah, she is."

Frank frowned at Joshua, then shook his head and smiled. "Would you like a cup of coffee? We've got some real coffee, not them ground-up acorns."

"Thanks. Yeah."

Frank called in the door . A few minutes later Carolyn brought out two cups of coffee.

"Carolyn, This here's Josh. He lives down the road, maybe you seen him."

"Yeah, I seen him. Never met him though. Hello, Josh."

"Hello."

She went back in the house.

Frank said, "Where'd you get wounded?

"In Tennessee. Chattanooga."

"Chattanooga? Damn, I was there too, at Missionary Ridge." Archer held up his hand. "That's where I left these fingers. Guess I shouldn't complain, a lotta guys died there, I coulda been one of 'em."

"I was at Lookout Mountain, the day before the Missionary Ridge fight. If I hadn't got shot when I did, we coulda ended up shootin' at each other."

"God, war is just so strange, so stupid. Seems like it all comes down to money."

"Yup, that's what it comes down to. I never agreed with the idea of Carolina seceding or with havin' a damn war, but the money men set the rules and then draft guys to go fight. But them fight? Hell no. If you had a plantation with more'n twenty slaves you could stay

55

home, make sure they were workin' your crop good."

"I didn't know that. I do know, on the Union side, if you paid three hundred bucks you could get outta the draft. The government was as hungry for money as it was for soldiers. But I didn't know that till it was too late, I was already in. And I didn't have that kinda money anyway."

"They sure know how to screw the little guy while they sit back home and sip their goddam tea."

"And count their goddam money."

When Josh left, Carolyn brought a cup of coffee for herself and refilled Frank's cup.

Frank asked "Did you know that guy before the war?"

"Yeah, seen him some, his place is just a piece down the road. He's got maybe ninety acres, grew cotton there before the war. He was married, but his wife Ellen, the fever took her back 'fore the war started. He got drafted into the army like pretty much all the men."

"Ever have any trouble with him?"

"No. Mind you, he did some lookin', but he kept his hands to hisself. Better'n some of the other white men round here."

"What do you mean?"

"I didn't have no trouble, Miz Fluker and her husband wouldn't stand for none of that stuff. But some of the other men that had slaves wasn't like that. Like Mister Shorter down the road, he had a coupla slave gals. When he and his friends played poker, the winner'd get to have his way with one of the gals. 'Course Shorter, he'd do that whenever he felt like it."

"Jesus."

"Yeah. His wife didn't like that none. One 'a those slave gals, Sheila, Miz Shorter tried to beat her with a broom handle one time, and Sheila wouldn't take it, took that broom right away from her. After that Miz Shorter tried to get her husband to sell Sheila, but of course he wouldn't. She's right good-lookin'.

56

"When the war got started, Shorter, he went in the army, there waren't nobody left on his farm but his wife, those gals, and a coupla field hands. Miz Shorter tried to sell Sheila down south again, but Sheila found out about it 'fore she could get it done, and she and the other gal and one of the hands, they ran off. Miz Shorter can't make the farm work without 'em, barely gettin' anythin' to eat from the garden."

Josh and Frank visited frequently that Spring. They talked about the war, how hard it was to get food, how slowly Carolina was recovering from its devastation, and their wounds.

Josh asked about Frank's hand.

"Mostly it's okay. Course there's a lot of things I can't do with it. Don't think I'll be pickin' a guitar any. How about your arm?"

"It's weird, it ain't even there but sometimes I get pain like it is, it's like my body still thinks it's there. And it reminds me 'bout when I got hit. I ended up lyin' on that mountain all that night, hurtin' like blazes, guys all around me, some dead, some hollerin' and groanin'. In the mornin' there was vultures all around, pickin' at dead guys."

"How long' were you lyin' there?"

"All night. In the mornin' the medics came through, put me on a stretcher. It didn't make any damn sense, medics from both sides, ours and the Union guys alongside each other, goin' through the battlefield pickin' up wounded. I mean, how stupid! The generals decide there's gonna be a cease-fire, so all of a sudden you stop shootin', send out the medics, pick up the busted soldiers, then the next day start shootin' each other again.

"And there were dead horses and mules, all over the place, hundreds of 'em. They were still lyin' there when I got out of the hospital, bloated and stinkin'. Some of 'em burst."

Frank nodded. "I saw the same stuff. Guess they got the guys' bodies buried quicker'n the horses, but it was still bad. My company pulled duty cleaning up around the hospitals, I still have nightmares about it. Blood all over the floors, guys screaming. Piles of arms and legs out on the ground, some of 'em with boots still on."

"Damn. The folks who decide it would be good to have a war don't think about shovelin' dead bodies into a hole."

"Or pieces of bodies."

And they talked about cotton. The South's economy was in tatters and the supply chain reaching New England and England couldn't begin to meet the demand. Whatever you grew got a good price. With the Fluker farm's two hundred acres, Frank had the land, but knew nothing about growing cotton. But Josh had grown up with it.

"Yeah, I know cotton pretty good, learned it from my daddy, grew it with him, then just myself 'fore I got drafted."

"Well I don't know shit about it. And this land, it's really different from around Buckeystown. The roads up there, they gotta curve and curl to get up the hills, ya just can't go straight up 'em. Down here they mostly don't have ta bend except to get over a river or a creek."

"You're right, but that makes plowin' and plantin' pretty easy, lotta straight lines. And damn few big rocks. It's good farmin' country, good cotton country."

"So, ya think I oughta learn how to grow cotton?"

"You got good land for it."

They came to a cooperative deal. Like almost all the South's mules and horses, Josh's mule had been commandeered, then died in the war, so he had no plow animal. But Frank had Goldie. Goldie'd never had a plow behind him but Josh figured he could teach him.

He did. Josh taught Frank cotton and Goldie plowed some of both farm's fields. Some, with the help of local ex-slaves who sharecropped—worked for a portion of the harvest—were plowed by hand. Carolyn helped with seeding and weeding, but when the first harvest came, thanks to plentiful rain, a good one, she was no longer in the fields. Her belly was swollen with their child.

January 2, 1866

> John Archer's first cries burst into the
> Carolina air. Despite Carolyn's brown
> skin, John's is as white as his father's.

Josh and Frank worked together through the growing season and fell
into an after-work routine, Josh visiting the Archers every Saturday
for supper. Widowed, Josh enjoyed the company and Carolyn's
cooking. After the baby arrived, Josh often sat in the easy chair in the
front room, John bouncing on his knee. He was now Uncle Josh.

During one of those meals, in late summer, he told them about
the local Klan.

"I'm afraid things is gettin' kinda nasty 'round Winnsboro. A
buncha war vets been meeting pretty regular, talkin' bad stuff about
colored folk and people who sympathize with 'em. They busted into a
nigra house northa here this week and beat the couple up pretty bad."

Carolyn nodded. "Yeah, I heard. Sheila, gal I know used to be
slave for the Shorters, she lives near there now. She told me, said
those guys wear white sheets, pointy hoods over their heads. Call
'emselves the Ku Klux. Some colored families is taken to sleepin'
out."

"Sleepin' out?" Frank asked.

"What the Ku Klux does is they ride up to a house, all dress up
like I said, and yell for the colored folks inside to come out.
Sometimes they shoot into the house. Up near Rock Hill, they been
doin' that almost every night. So what folks been doin' is take a
blanket and go sleep in the woods. Ku Klux don't know where to find
'em if they ain't in a house. The folks go back home when day comes,
cause it only happens at night."

Frank said, "How'd you hear about it, Josh?"

"Some of the folks who's doin' it used to be friends of mine.

59

They know I been workin' some with you, so they ain't real high on me anymore. And for that matter, I ain't real high on them, just don't believe in that crap. I don't hang around with any of 'em, and they pretty much don't talk to me, but I still hear stuff down at Hilliard's farm store, some of 'em braggin' how they're keepin' the niggers in their place.

"I said some to Mark Nicholas down at Hilliard's 'bout how you're just a veteran, screwed over fightin' a war jes' like we were, but he don't see it that way. You're a damn Yankee and you shouldn't be here. So now I don't say nothin' to nobody, jes' buy our stuff and go. And we gotta keep doin' it like we been doin' it, I'll buy what we need, you don't show yer face in there.

"And I hate to say it, but if folks see us spendin' time together like this, it ain't good. We probly shouldn't be doin' it every weekend like we been, and not get together till after dark."

"That sure stinks. We'll miss spendin' easy time with you."

"I'm gonna miss it too, gonna miss seeing baby John. Guess he'll be in bed."

"You think me and Carolyn's in any danger from that Klan stuff?"

"I dunno. But you damn well better keep your rifle loaded. And your shotgun."

Carolyn brought out dessert. They ate the cream custard pie in silence.

Lying in bed that evening, Frank turned to Carolyn.

"Whaddya think about what Josh said about the Klan? You hear anything from your friends that make you feel like there's danger?"

"Like I said, there's some bad things happened 'round Rock Hill, but I ain't heard nothin' goin' on down here. 'Course it's not like I hear everythin'."

"Y'know, we could always move up to Maryland, to my folks' place, like we talked about."

60

"Yeah, I remember."

"Let's get through this season. If things don't look good then, maybe we'll go up there."

Carolyn turned on her side and was soon asleep, but Frank lay awake, staring at the ceiling.

> *Damn, there's times I wish I wasn't*
> *down here, wish I never heard of cotton.*
> *No matter what happens, I'm gonna get*
> *us outta here soon as we sell this crop.*

It was close to midnight before he fell asleep.

November 22, 1866

> Blessed by a good growing season, not
> too much nor too little rain, the cotton is
> waist-high. Frank and Josh anticipate an
> even better crop than last year.

The Archers had finished supper, put the baby down for the night, and were on the front porch swing. Katydids were trilling, the brilliant moon was just clearing the horizon. Frank heard rustling in the bushes on one side of the porch.

He stood up. "Think we got a rabbit, Carolyn."

A man wearing a white hood stood up with a rifle. "You set back down, mister, and stay there or you're a dead man."

Frank sat. The man whistled. A dozen men on horseback, all in sheets and hoods, rode into the front yard.

"You havin' a good night, Archer? Enjoyin' yourself, niggerlover?"

Frank's rifle was leaning in a corner of the living room. He'd have to leave Carolyn alone on the porch if he ran for it, but anyhow, what good could one man with a rifle do against a dozen? They'd shoot him before he got through the front door.

Half of them dismounted and came up on the porch. Some stood in front of Frank, guns pointed at him.

One growled at Carolyn. "Well, ain't you purty, little nigger lady. Probly right good spreadin' your legs for that man, too, huh? He come all the way down here from up north just to find you, you must be good. Let's us just see how good!"

He grabbed Carolyn's arm, pulled her off the swing. Frank jumped up, a rifle barrel smashed the side of his head, and he fell to the floor.

Carolyn screamed, "No, please, please, don't hurt him. I'll do anything, don't hurt him!"

"You're damn right you'll do anything." A second man took her other arm. They pulled her off the porch, into the darkness at the side of the house. Half a dozen followed them.

As Frank lay on the porch two men stood on his wrists. Another ripped his shirt off his back, another brandished a horsewhip. "Here's what you shoulda got when you come down here, Yankee. It's comin' late, but by god it's comin'."

The first stroke of the whip raised a welt on Frank's back. The second and the third, more welts. He strained to get his legs under him, was kicked in the stomach and fell again. Whip strokes now brought blood. Again and again and again they came.

He groaned, "Carolyn." He heard no reply, just men shouting and mumbling from the side of the house. Then he heard nothing and could no longer feel the lash.

Slowly Frank regained consciousness. At first, there were no sounds. Then, the katydids. Splinters in the porch floor stabbed his cheek. He remembered where he was. His belly throbbed, his back burned furiously. Blood pooled sticky on the porch around him, under his arms, around his belly. He remembered the whip. Then he remembered it all.

He tried to speak, but only a croak came. He tried again. "Ca. Caro. Carolyn."

No sound but the katydids. He raised his head. The horses and men were gone. Groaning, he pulled his knees beneath him, spread his arms through the sticky blood, raised his body first on elbows, then hands.

"Carolyn!"

He got one leg up, tried to stand. Dizziness spun his head, he fell. He crawled to the edge of the porch, rolled onto his side, swung his legs onto the porch steps. He reached up, grabbed the railing, pulled himself upright, staggered down the steps calling.

"Carolyn!"

She lay naked on her back in the grass, clothes torn and scattered near her. He groaned as he knelt beside her. "Carolyn, Carolyn."

The moonlight showed darkness on her belly, on her thighs. He touched it. Blood. He bent down, put his ear against her breast. Her heart was beating. She was breathing. He clenched his teeth against the pain as he picked her up, staggered to the porch, up the steps. He kicked the front door open, laid her on the front room couch, covered her with a blanket.

"Carolyn." Her eyes fluttered open, turned to him.

"Frank, are you alright?"

"Yes, I'm okay." Tears poured down his cheeks. "I'm gonna get you a doctor."

She nodded, closed her eyes.

Teeth clenched against the pain, Frank staggered down the steps and, staying off the road, limped as fast as he could to Josh's.

He banged on the front door. "Josh, Josh, open up! Josh!"

A lamp lit in Josh's bedroom at the top of the steps. He came down in pajamas, hurried to the door.

"Carolyn, it's Carolyn, she's hurt, she needs a doctor!"

Josh looked at his bloody friend on the porch, thought my god, if she needs a doctor worse than him, it must be awful. He pulled on pants and shoes and they walked to the Archer's house, Frank limping badly.

Carolyn's eyes were open now. She stared at the ceiling in silence.

Josh shook his head. "I'll go get Doctor Arleigh, he'll come, he took care of Ellen when she got sick. You stay here with her."

He ran down the steps, around to the barn, saddled Goldie and galloped toward Columbia.

Frank sat beside Carolyn holding her hand. She'd closed her eyes. A streak of blood smeared her cheek. Time crawled, to him it felt like the clock had stopped as he sat and waited.

"Do you hurt bad, Carolyn?"

She didn't reply. It was two hours, the longest two hours in his life, before the doctor came. As he examined her, Josh and Frank sat on the porch. Frank related the night's horror.

Josh shook his head slowly. "Jesus, Jesus, I didn't know, I didn't know, nobody told me anything. I guess they figured I might warn you or something. They didn't say a damn thing to me. I mean, I hear some of the things they say, but they say a lot of stuff they don't actually do. I'm so, so sorry."

"I know."

"What're you gonna do?"

"I don't know."

Doctor Arleigh came out on the porch.

"I think she's gonna be okay. She's been raped, and her private parts are torn up some, but the bleeding has stopped. There's no other damage I can see, at least not to her body. She's not talking, just says a few words, yes and no if I ask her something. We'll have to wait and see what happens with her mind. I'll come by again in the morning, see if she should go to the hospital. I don't think the Columbia hospital will take her because she's colored, but the Northern army's got a sickbay set up, maybe she could go there.

"Mister Archer, come on inside where there's light and I'll take a look at you. Josh, could you get some water so we can get this blood off him."

In the front room, the doctor used rags to wash Frank's back, then dry it.

"Frank, have you got any whiskey? You can have a drink if that'll make you feel better, but what I've found with cuts like these is washing them with whiskey helps keep them from getting infected."

Frank pointed past Josh. "Josh, there's a bottle of whiskey in a cabinet in the kitchen."

Josh brought the whiskey. Frank took a big slug.

Doctor Arleigh took the bottle, poured it liberally on a piece of cloth. "Now this is going to hurt a bit."

Frank nodded, gritted his teeth as the doctor wiped the lacerations with whiskey.

The sun's first rays shone through the front room's windows and Josh, asleep on the floor, heard John call from his upstairs bedroom. By some miracle, one could argue a blessed one, year-old John had slept through the entire nightmarish night. Carolyn lay silent on the couch, Frank leaning against it.

Josh stood, walked to the stairs. "I'll go get him, you just stay there, take it easy."

He went in John's room, reached down into his crib. "Mornin' boy. We're gonna get you some breakfast over my house, okay? Your mom and dad aren't feelin' so good."

He dressed John, carried him downstairs. "We'll just let your mom and dad sleep, they're tired out."

They walked to Josh's house and shared a breakfast of scrambled eggs. Josh's lead field hand Sam called through the kitchen screen door.

"Mornin', mista Josh. We gonna be choppin' today?"

"Mornin' Sam. Yeah, we'll be choppin', but first we got a young man needs some takin' care of. Think your lady friend Cheri could come by and stay with John here for awhile? Or mebbe take him back to your place?"

"Well, I figger so. I'll go git 'er."

Later that morning, Frank and Josh sat outside the Union army hospital tent. Carolyn lay inside on her side, legs curled up, arms between them, pain allayed by tincture of opium. Doctor Arleigh and the army doctor were cautiously optimistic in their prognosis of her physical condition, but concerned that she still said little more than yes and no in response to questions. She was to stay at the hospital until at least the next day. Arleigh and the army doc had examined Frank's back and saw no need for further treatment yet.

"So, it looks like she's gonna be alright, don't you think, Frank? Sounds like that's what the doctors are telling us."

Sitting rigidly upright, Frank grimaced in pain as he replied. "I guess so. I sure wish she'd talk more."

"Well, maybe she'll be doin' better tomorrow. I think the best thing for us to do now is go home. You need to rest, give that back a chance to heal. I'll be by tomorrow, we'll see how things are goin' then."

With a groan, Frank stood. They walked to where Goldie was tethered. Frank couldn't lift his mounting leg high enough to reach a stirrup, so Josh bent under his butt and stood, taking Frank's weight on his shoulder so he could mount.

Half an hour later, they sat on Frank's front porch.

"I'm so damn sorry, Frank. I just didn't know."

"Y'already said that."

"Yeah. Look, there's no way you're gonna be able to work your crop. Me and my nigras will do it, you just go in, go to bed and heal up. I'll stop by in the mornin' and we'll go check on Carolyn. Cheri's takin' good care of John."

Frank nodded, slowly stood. "Thanks for doin' what you could. It waren't your fault, I know."

He stood, went in the house and lay down.

Josh came by early the next two mornings and they visited the army hospital together. Carolyn's physical condition slowly improved but she still lay in fetal position in near-silence. After their visit on the second day they sat on Frank's front porch steps, Frank stiffly upright. Though his back was healing it was still too painful to sit on anything with a back, like the swing.

Josh said, "So whaddya think you wanna do? You wanna try to do anythin' legal about what happened?"

"I don't think so. Yeah, you got a pretty good idea of who they were, at least some of 'em, but they's no way to prove that. And if you got involved, you could be the next one to get whipped."

Josh nodded. "Yeah."

"I don't see any choice but to get the hell out of here. If we stay, it could happen again, anytime. I think me and Carolyn should go north to my folks in Maryland."

"What about your place? What about your crop?"

"Been thinkin' about that. How'd you feel about renting the place from me? Goldie too. Tween her and your hands I think you could handle your fields plus mine. With the price of cotton these days, you should be able to make good money, enough to pay me rent, your costs, probly put some away."

They came to an agreement. Josh would rent, would sent a check monthly to Frank in Maryland. Frank wrote his parents and let them know he and the family were coming. He didn't tell them the horrible details of why.

****

Two weeks later, Josh and Frank sat on the front seat of the farm wagon, John between them. Carolyn lay in the back of the wagon on a mattress. It would take them two days to reach the Southern Railroad station in Rock Hill. Josh knew the road well, had traveled it to sell their cotton market and buy seed and farm equipment. If you pushed hard, you could make the trip from Winnsboro in one long day, but with Carolyn lying in the back of the wagon, they couldn't push hard.

On his previous trips, Josh had sometimes overnighted with the Ainslees, a family that took in lodgers. They stayed a night with the Ainslees on this trip. Martha and Homer Ainslee also had a one-year-old, a girl named Sherry. John and Sherry crawled on the floor together, but showed little interest in each other. When they met again, years later, that would not be the case.

December 9, 1866

Maryland

It took two more days for trains to take the Archers from Rock Hill to Frederick. Isabel and Robert, Frank's parents, met them at the station and took them by buggy to the Buckeystown farm. Carolyn was still very quiet, but in time regained a semblance of normality in the peace of the farm. The family doctor examined her when she first arrived. He said she had healed well from the rape, but it was unlikely she and Frank would have any more children.

Isabel introduced her to embroidery—needlepoint and crewel—and the disciplined, repetitive movements of the needle were therapy for her traumatized mind and body. As time went on, she resumed many of the activities that'd kept her busy at the Fluker's. She worked in the garden with Isabel and became friends with the McAllisters, who rented the tenant house on the farm.

Robert was thrilled to have his son helping on the farm. When he and Frank were in the fields, Carolyn, Isabel and Darlene McAllister spent time together embroidering, talking and cooking. The two families often ate together on weekends.

John

As John grew he took particular interest in the animals: the horses, cattle and sheep. If a lamb was rejected by its mother, or for some other reason found itself an orphan, it wasn't unusual to find him in the barn with a bottle of milk. More than once he slept in the hay with a lamb.

He learned quickly about animal health from his grandfather, from the veterinarian who visited the farm occasionally, and from the farrier who trimmed their two horses' hooves. Since the horses spent virtually no time on paved surfaces, horseshoes weren't needed, just trimming. By the time he was 15, he'd taken over most of the farrier work, doing all the routine hoof trimming, the farrier called only if there was an unusual problem. And he adapted some of what he learned about horse hooves to the sheep. He found that trimming and cleaning a sheep's hoof, then treating it with a copper compound, would often cure foot rot.

He rode horseback to school in Frederick, but his schoolwork was uneven. He got good grades in the sciences, but barely passed English and history. And he didn't graduate.

Buckeystown wasn't Carolina, but it certainly wasn't free of racial prejudice. In his sophomore year, Roger Odum accosted him as school was letting out. Odum was two years his senior, three or four inches taller than John and heavier.

"Hey Archer, how you doin?"

"Okay I guess."

"Y'know what I hear? I hear you don't belong here at this school. It ain't for niggers."

John didn't reply, pulled his saddle from the roofed saddle rack and walked toward his horse.

"Ya thought nobody'd know, huh? Well, we know. We know your mama's a nigger."

John slung the saddle over his horse's back, cinched it, fed the

69

bit into the horse's mouth and mounted.

"And we don't want no niggers here. It's against the law."

As John rode away, he spoke back over his shoulder, "Well, I don't wanna be here."

The next morning Frank came out to the barn. John was picking one of the horses' hooves.

"Hey, how come you're not in school?"

"They found out Mom is colored. I can't go there any more.

Hands on hips, Frank frowned. "How'd they find out?"

"Who knows? People talk."

"Yeah, they do. They do. Y'know, I think there's a Black school in the county, you could go there."

"I don't think so. Think I've had enough of school. Had enough of these darn people. I'm learnin' plenty here on the farm. Granpa's got lots of books, I can read them."

John set the hoof down, pulled another onto his thigh and started picking it.

"Okay, I guess," Frank said. "I'm goin' out to look at the hay field. Lemme know if you change your mind, we'll figure somethin' out."

John didn't change his mind.

April 2, 1880

Thirteen years have passed since the Archers left Winnsboro. The cotton farm has prospered and, true to his word, Josh has sent Frank rent checks every month, the check usually accompanied with a note about what's happening on the farm. The note that comes with the April check brings

70

exceptional news. He's met a local gal, a woman who'd lost her husband in the war. They're planning on getting married and he'd be mighty happy if Frank will do him the honor of being his best man when he marries Corinne in June.

Sitting at the kitchen table, Frank showed the letter to Carolyn.

"Y'know, I'd really like to see him again, and it'd be great to be his best man. Whaddya think?"

Carolyn sighed, eyes roaming the ceiling. Her lips moved as if words were assembling themselves in her mouth, reluctant to escape.

"Well Carolyn, whaddya think? You wanna go?"

"I jes' doan think I can do it. It's wonderful Josh feels that way, it is. But I doan wanna see South Carolina ever again."

"I know, I know. Would you mind if I went without you?"

"No, I guess that'd be awright. You think you'd be safe?"

"I'm pretty sure I would. Josh wouldn't have asked me to come if things were nasty now."

"I guess not."

"You wouldn't be lonely, right, with Mom and the other folks here?"

"No, I'll miss you but I won't be too lonely. Long as you're not gone too long."

That evening, as Frank was writing Josh to confirm his plans, John came in from grooming the horses.

"Who you writing, Dad?"

"Our friend Josh, the fella who's farming our land down in Winnsboro. I'm gonna go down and visit him awhile, he's getting married."

"What's Josh like?"

"He's a decent, honest man. He was wounded in the war, lost an arm, but he gets along fine without it, the farm's doin' well. We worked together awhile before we came up here, and got to be good friends."

"How long you gonna be gone?"

"Oh, I guess a week, maybe a little more. Not more'n two weeks."

John hesitated. "Could I go with you?"

"So Buckeystown's not good enough for you, eh? Gettin' too big for this little country place?"

"No, no, it'd just be nice to take a trip, go somewhere, see someplace other than Buckeystown for a little while. And I was so young when we left Winnsboro, I really don't remember it. It'd be nice to know more about where I was born."

Frank studied his son. Fourteen, with his father's blue eyes and a mop of blond hair, he was well-muscled from farm work, nearly his father's height. His skin gave no hint of his mother's color.

"Y'know, there's some things about where you were born that ain't so nice. You remember what I told you about those scars on my back. There's still people down there that do that kinda stuff."

"Do you think it'd be safe?"

"Yeah. I wouldn't go if I didn't."

"So, can I go?"

"I'll talk to your mother."

Carolyn was not happy when Frank told her John wanted to accompany him to Winnsboro.

"Bad enough you're goin' down there, why do you wanna take John?"

"It wasn't my idea, it was his. He wants to see where he was born. And he doesn't have the awful memories we do. We won't be there long, maybe a week, we'll be back before you know it."

"I still doan' like it."

"We'll be careful, and we'll be with Josh the whole time."

72

June 12, 1880

Carolyn reluctantly agreed, and as Frank and John step from the train at the Winnsboro station, Josh Ranson, waving his hat in the crowd, rushes forward. His eyes gleam, he wraps his arm around Frank.

"Been a long time, my friend. It's wonderful to see you!"

"And to see you, my friend. You haven't aged hardly a bit."

"Ha! And who's this strapping young man behind you? Couldn't be John, could it?"

"Who else?"

Josh took John's hand. "Time sure does fly, young man. Last time I saw you, you'd barely learned to walk. Welcome back to Winnsboro."

"Thanks. It's good to be back."

Josh pointed at the dirt lot alongside the station where horses were hitched to a rail alongside several buggies. "The wagon's right over there, toss your bags in and we'll go have ya meet Corinne."

As the buggy rattled to the farm, John was amazed by the acres and acres of cotton alongside the road. "Wow, so that's cotton, it's really pretty."

"I guess it is, but I don't usually think of it like that. When I look at it I see work. And somethin' that pays the bills."

They pulled to a stop in front of the Ranson farmhouse. As Frank and John pulled their suitcases from the wagon Josh hitched the horse to the rail.

"Welcome to our humble home, my friends. C'mon in and meet my beautiful lady."

Corinne had a pot of coffee ready, and they sat at the kitchen table sipping. Sam, Josh's lead hand, knocked on the screen door, opened it.

"C'mon in Sam. You remember these fellas?"

"Well, d'one I do, good to see you Mistuh Frank. But that other one, if you han't told me he's comin' I sure wouldn't know him. He's a heap bigger'n last he was here."

"John, you probly don't remember Sam, but he 'n his lady Cheri took care of you some when you were down here. Sam, John seems interested in our cotton. Why doncha take him out, show him some of the tools we use workin' with it."

"Be glad to, Mistah Josh. John, c'mon out and I'll show you how we does it."

The screen door slammed behind Sam and John.

"So, I'm really glad the farm's been goin' well, and I thank you for all those checks." Frank said.

"Happy to do it, and glad the farm's been workin'. You know what farmin's like, sometimes you work your butt off and the weather or somethin' else, bugs or blight or whatever, it kills yer crop anyhow. And you don't know how much you'll get for your cotton from one year to the next. A few years ago we were gettin' eighteen cents a pound, now the price's down to half that."

Frank: "Yeah, I been seein' cotton prices goin' up and down in the paper. And been seein' a bit of the news down here, the elections and all. Sounds like it ain't been an easy time, this fella Wade Hampton and the RedShirts."

"Yeah, it ain't been an easy time. Hampton's one of the old names down here, owns five plantations and hundreds of slaves, least he used to. He was a general in the cavalry during the war, fought at a bunch of the battles, his brother was killed in one of 'em. And he was wounded a buncha times himself."

"He was governor for awhile, wasn't he?"

"Yeah, he got elected in '76, but nobody really knows if he shoulda been. In two of the counties west of here, the vote count for him was bigger'n the total number of votes cast. You wonder how the hell that can be?"

"Sure doesn't make sense."

"That election got really nasty. The Klan, the RedShirts, and groups they call rifle clubs—I know some of those guys—got violent, there was a buncha lynchings. A lot of it was 'cause the coloreds had got the vote, and they were voting. Over in Hamburg, there was a battle between the colored National Guard company and some white militia guys. Nobody really won the battle, but the day after it, that militia dragged a buncha coloreds down by the Savannah River, picked out five and shot 'em."

"I did see that in the paper. One of 'em was an elected representative, wasn't he?"

"Yeah, name was Simon Coker. They shot him in the head while he was prayin'. Guy named 'Pitchfork' Ben Tillman and about ninety other guys got charged with those murders, but none of 'em been prosecuted."

They sat in silence for several minutes. Frank spoke.

"I didn't know it was so bad. How do colored folks keep livin' down here?"

"Well, it's not so bad now. They sent federal troops down, and everything's quieted down. And Hampton's not governor any more. Now he's a US senator."

"That's not so bad?"

"Guess that depends how you look at it. At least things are quiet now."

Four days later, Josh waves from the platform of the Winnsboro station as the northbound train pulls out. From a window, John and Frank wave back. The day before, Frank had beamed as Josh slid a wedding ring on Corinne's hand at the Convent Baptist Church. Reverend Collington, who'd refused to marry him and Carolyn fifteen years before, performed the ceremony. Collington showed no sign of recognizing Frank, and Frank did nothing to refresh his memory.

1884

Buckeystown

> As his teen years pass, John grows restless. High school is over, and the farm work isn't keeping him busy. He enjoys it, but he really isn't needed. His father and his grandfather—despite his age, still vital and strong—are quite capable of doing all that needs to be done on the place.

He and Frank were in the barn at the end of a workday, repairing a broken spoke on a wagon wheel.

"What was it like growing cotton, dad?"

"Well, it's an interesting crop. It grows well in Carolina, but like almost any crop, ya never know how good a year's harvest will be. Depends on weather and bugs, things you can't control. Sometimes you make good money, sometimes not. But you pretty much always break even, have enough to pay the bills. Josh's had some real good years, he's been able to put money in the bank.

"But on top of bugs and weather, now there's competition. Josh tells me they're growin' a buncha cotton in Texas now, and that's pushing the market price down."

"How do you sell it?"

"Josh takes his crop up to Rock Hill. It's been a cotton market for awhile. Back when I grew it all the cotton was shipped to England or New England to be made into fabric, but that's changing. Rock Hill's on the railroad line, that helps a lot, and a few years ago it got a cotton mill, the first one in the state. It's steam-powered, they call it the Rock Hill Cotton Factory. And there's a couple more in Carolina."

"So the South's finally catchin' up, huh?"

"Yeah, in some ways. In others it's got a long way to go."

They sat in silence awhile.

"Dad, I think I'd like to go grow some cotton."

"Cotton? In Winnsboro?"

"Yeah. You don't really need me up here, it's about time I got to livin' my own life."

"You got cotton in your blood, huh? Must be somethin' about bein' born in Carolina."

"Well, I don't see it when I bleed, but I guess it's there. You think Josh could teach me about growin' it?"

"I guess he could. He taught me, so I figger he could teach you. You really wanna go?"

"Yeah."

" I'll talk to your mom. Don't know if she'll be real happy about you goin' off, especially to Carolina. But if she says it's okay, I'll write Josh and see if he'd like another hand."

Winnsboro

Josh has sold his Winnsboro house, but not his land, and he and Corinne have moved into Carolyn's house. He replies enthusiastically to Frank's letter, and John, with Carolyn's reluctant agreement, is now with them, learning all about planting, fertilizing and harvesting cotton. A strong eighteen-year-old, he copes well with early mornings and long workdays alongside Sam and Josh's five sharecroppers.

Early one morning he was in the field chopping cotton—weeding and thinning the emerging plants—when Josh's voice screamed from the storage shed. "John, John, come here!"

John dashed to the shed to find Josh sitting on the dirt floor with blood spurting from a deep cut on his arm. John squeezed above the cut.

"What happened?"

"I was sharpening that scythe and the damn blade broke loose from the handle and flipped against my arm."

"Damn, it sure is cut." Sam had heard Josh's scream too and was at the shed door. "Sam, grab one of those old shirts from the shelf and cut an arm off of it."

Sam slashed the arm off and John wrapped it around Josh's arm just above the elbow. Using a wood scrap as a handle, he twisted it tight. The improvised tourniquet slowed the blood flow, then stopped it.

"How's it feel, Josh? Too tight?"

"Yeah, it's pretty damn tight. Has it gotta be like that?"

"For now, yeah. We'll loosen it periodically so you still get blood in that arm, but not so much this cut starts bleedin' again. Think you can stand up?"

"I think so." John held Josh's good arm and he stood, wobbling.

John: "Let's go in the house, take a bit of a break."

They walked to the house, opened the kitchen door. Corinne was cooking greens.

"My god, Josh, what happened to you?"

She listened to the story as she poured glasses of water for the men.

"Well Josh, looks like you got a good excuse to take a break from work for awhile. You go lie down in the bed and rest. Wait a minute, let me get more of the blood off you, we doan' want it on the sheets."

John held Josh's arm off the table as she washed blood from his elbow and forearm with a wet rag. The flow of blood had stopped completely.

He said, "I'm goin' back out to work, but I'll come back once in a while and loosen up that tourniquet. You lie down, keep that arm up. It'll bleed worse if you let it hang down."

Corinne held Josh's arm as he walked back to the bedroom. "Here's a good clean rag, you hold it over that cut. Don't want you bleedin' on the sheets, do we?"

Back at the shed, John picked up the scythe blade that had slashed Josh. It had snapped at its junction with the handle. He pulled a handful of cotton from a bale in the shed, wiped Josh's blood from the blade and the grinding wheel stand and threw the cotton in a trash bucket. His hand was smeared with Josh's blood. He pulled more cotton from the bale and wiped it clean.

He returned to Josh's room an hour later. Corinne watched as he loosened the tourniquet, waited, retightened it. When he loosened the device, the blood came more slowly than before, but late in the afternoon, it still hadn't stopped completely. Whenever the tourniquet was loosened, blood oozed.

"Well, it's not clotting completely. Corinne, you got yarrow in the garden, don't you?"

"Yes."

"Could you get some and grind it up fine?"

Ten minutes later John applied a handful of ground yarrow to Josh's wound and wrapped it in place with a rag.

"Looks like we're gonna have to start calling you Doctor John, huh," Corinne said.

"Well, you better wait and see if this works before you start doin' that."

"How'd you learn about this stuff?"

"We've got a good many animals on the Maryland farm, and I learned a lot from my dad and the vet who took care of them. People aren't the only animals who bleed. Sometimes vets use tourniquets on horses and other animals."

"How'd you learn about yarrow?"

"There's still some Tuscarora Indians up in the west part of Virginia, a few in Maryland where our farm is, and we got to know one of 'em. Wallace Anderson, they call him 'Mad Bear.' I cut myself once when we were cutting twigs and branches for a campfire, I was just a kid. He used yarrow on my cut and it stopped the bleeding just like that!"

He snapped his fingers. "Let's see how it works on Josh. Josh, you hold that arm still, don't let it hang down alongside the bed, keep it up by your head."

After supper they loosened the tourniquet again and no new blood came.

"Well it's lookin' pretty good. Corinne, you know how to work that tourniquet—before you go to sleep, loosen it one more time and see if any new blood comes. If it does, give me a holler. If if doesn't, just put it on half-tight and check to see if there's any new bleeding. If not, that should take him through the night. We gotta keep that arm workin', seein's how it's his only good one."

At the "doctor's" insistence, Josh didn't do any work for the next three or four days. His arm healed.

The weather is kind to the farm's crop that year, and they take nearly three hundred bales to the Rock Hill market in the Fall. The next year is even better, just short of four hundred bales. But despite their success, something in John doesn't feel satisfied. You can make a living growing cotton, yes, but aside from paying the bills, he doesn't find much meaning in it. Is growing cotton really what his life's going to be about? Cotton farming? And the work's grueling.

80

He'd made up his mind. One November evening when supper was done he leaned back from the table.

"Josh, let's get a glass of that rum we been savin' and go sit on the porch. Somethin' I'd like to talk to you about."

Corinne was putting the last of the dishes in the sink. "You men go 'head get your rum, I'll deal with the dishes."

They settled on the porch. John sipped his rum.

"Y'know, I like workin' with you just fine, and I'm really glad the place is doin' well, but I just don't think I'm cut out to be a farmer."

"Y'don't huh. Well, tell ya the truth, I kinda knew your heart wasn't in it. Mebbe should say cotton isn't in your blood. So what is? In your blood, I mean."

"Well, there was a time when Dad accused me of havin' cotton in my blood, but it seems he was wrong. I want to be a doctor."

Frank frowned. "So, your healin' my arm's gone to your head, has it? No, no, I'm just teasin'. You really think that?"

"Yeah, I really do. And by some kind of miracle, there's a medical school close by, in Charleston. It's kind of amazing, there aren't many medical colleges in the whole country, and one of 'em, the South Carolina College of Medicine, is only a hundred miles from here. I hear really good things about it."

"So. I got a feelin' you got more to say."

John laughed. "Yeah, I do. How'd you like to stop payin' my dad rent and just buy this farm?"

Josh raised his eyebrows. "Buy you out, huh? You talk to your dad about this idea?"

"Yeah, I did. I wrote him last month and he says that'd be fine with him. He and Mom are happy where they are, and he said if I didn't want to farm it, he'd be glad to sell to you."

"Mmm, I'm glad to hear that. Y'know, I been pretendin' to the local guys that this whole place is mine, been doin' that 'cause they wouldn't be happy if they knew I was rentin' from a damn Yankee. Be good not to have to pretend any more."

John grinned. "So, how do we do it?"

"I sure wish I could talk to him face to face, but that ain't gonna happen. Guess we can swap telegrams and figger out a price. There's a telegraph office in Winnsboro."

Christmas Day, 1885

John's been admitted to the South Carolina College of Medicine and will begin classes early in January. The friends sit down for what they know will be their last meal together for awhile. Corinne's fixed a real Christmas feast. Ham (theirs), hominy, collards and a six-layer cake with chocolate icing. The farm's sale has gone through, and Frank has transferred part of the sale price into a bank account for John. It will be plenty to see him through medical school and renting a place in Charleston while he studies.

After supper, John and Josh sat again on the front porch with rum, this time with Corinne. They leaned together, clinked glasses.

"Here's to Doctor Archer!"

1886

The war hadn't been kind to South Carolina or Charleston. Nor had nature or fortune. At the end of 1861, a massive fire, apparently started accidentally, destroyed 164 acres of the city and damaged the College of Medicine. In 1863 the Federals had begun a siege and bombardment which continued throughout the war. When Confederate President Davis visited the city in November of that year, he described it as "a heap of ruins."

The College of Medicine suspended classes during the war, but is fully functional in January of 1886 when John moves into a Charleston boarding house between the college and Roper Hospital. He loves learning medicine and finds most of his classes fascinating, particularly the physiology courses taught by Professor Michel. He's surprised to find colored men at the school. One, Dr. A.C. McClennan, is an occasional lecturer. Another, Moses Camplin, is a fellow student.

He focuses intensely on his studies, spending little time in Charleston's bars, and volunteers his services at Roper Hospital. It had opened in 1856, subsidized by the city to treat "sick, maimed and diseased paupers . . . without regard of complexion, religion or nation." During the War it had served as a Confederate hospital and prison for Union soldiers.

The hospital still deals with the consequences of the War. Nearly a quarter of South Carolina's men had died in it, and another quarter were injured, many with amputated limbs. John's first patient one morning is a grizzled man with a wooden leg, wearing a battered Confederate cap.

"Good morning sir. How can I help you?"

"This damn leg don't fit good, it keeps rubbin' a sore on me."

"Well, take it off and let's take a look."

He unbuckled the straps that held his prosthetic on and pulled back the folded pant leg that cushioned its junction with his thigh. His leg had been amputated just above the knee, and the scar at the amputation is red and inflamed.

"Well, I can see that it hurts. More padding would help."

"I sure hope so."

John cleaned the skin with a carbolic acid solution. As he was searching through a storage cabinet for something to serve as padding, the man spoke.

"You don't sound like you're from here. Where you from?"

"Well I was born close to here, in Winnsboro, but we moved away when I was barely more than a baby."

"Where'd you move to?"

"Maryland."

The man grimaced. "Thought so. How come you're back here?

"Well, it's a little complicated. I came back to farm a place we owned in Winnsboro, but it turned out I wasn't a great farmer, or maybe I just found I didn't want to be a farmer. But farming for awhile gave me time to figure out what I did want to be."

"A doctor, huh?"

John nodded. "Yes, I finally figured it out. Ah, here it is."

He pulled a roll of soft cotton fabric from the cabinet, cut a length from it and folded into a pad.

"Try this under that scar. It'll spread the weight out some, should ease the hurting."

He handed the rest of the roll to the man and poured some of the carbolic acid mixture into a jar.

"And take this, once a day clean the scar with it."

The man strapped his leg back on, putting the pad between it and his stump. "Yeah, I guess that does feel some better. Thanks."

"You're welcome. And if it continues to give you trouble, come back and see me."

John's grades for the first semester were excellent. He was encouraged by compliments from his professors as the school's summer session began. It was a session that would change his life dramatically.

Sherry

August 31, 1886

Shortly before 10 in the evening, John is studying for final exams, hunched over an anatomy book in a hardback chair. His room on the second floor of the boarding house is lit by a flickering oil lamp. He hears a low rumbling, then he feels it. His chair shakes, a pen holder on his desk rocks, tips over. The picture on the wall above the desk rattles, crashes to the floor. He's never felt anything like this before, but knows what it has to be.

An earthquake.

He dropped the book, grabbed the lamp, ran to the door and down the steps into the street. The ground shook. A chimney on the house next door collapsed, bricks bouncing onto the street in a cloud of dust. Down the street, a horse screamed and reared, throwing itself on its side, toppling the carriage it was pulling.

A tower at Roper Hospital collapsed, bringing down part of its front wall and blocking the main entrance. John ran to the hospital, groped his way by the lamp's light through plaster dust and smoke to a side door. Inside, he crawled over a fallen wall to a patient ward. The first two patients he found lay dead in their beds, covered with debris. He followed the sound of a groan to a bed with a man writhing, one arm pinned under a fallen roof beam. He grabbed the beam, tried to lift it.

As he strained, unable to budge the beam, a woman, carrying another light, crunched her way across the ward's fallen plaster. She extended a broken piece of timber, part of a wall stud, toward him.

"A lever might work, try this."

He stuck one end under the fallen beam and lifted. It barely moved.

"Let me get on it." She bent, put her shoulder under the stud. "Okay, together!"

The stud lifted a couple of inches. The patient slid from beneath it, fell to the floor, his forearm bent and bleeding.

"We've got to get him out of here. Is any part of the building still intact?" John said.

"I saw staff taking wounded into the wash-house next door. We can take him there."

She picked up the lanterns. John raised the man, groaning, wrapped his good arm around his neck and half-carried him to the hallway. At the back of the corridor, flames flickered. "Oh god, it's on fire."

In the wash-house, among the big sinks and piles of laundry, patients lay on the floor, were propped against the walls. Some were crying, some staring wide-eyed at nothing. A medical student and a nurse moved among them, working to stop bleeding, propping heads on folded wash-house rags.

In the light of the lamps she held, John now saw his helper well. She was young, slender, tall. Her black hair hung sweat-soaked around her dust-coated face. Plaster dust covered her dress. A nurse's dress. She was probably a student in the nursing school.

"I'm goin' back in the building," John said.

"I'll go with you."

They scrambled over debris into the hallway, struggled down it toward the still-flickering flames to another ward. Its door was intact but the wall alongside it had collapsed. A leg extended from the wall's wreckage. John and the girl tore at the plaster and lath blanketing the body, uncovering the torso, wearing a nurse's uniform. Then the face.

"Oh no!" The girl screamed as she knelt by the still body, lifted the head, brushed dirt from the face. Dulled with plaster dust, her eyes stared unseeing.

"Jessica!"

"You know her?"

She sobbed. "Oh god, oh god yes. She's my roommate."

John knelt beside the body, put his ear to the chest. He shook his head. "I'm sorry."

An aftershock rumbled through the building. Dust flew into the air. In the next room, he heard a crash as a wall or rafter collapsed. "We've got to get out of here."

Tears streaming down her cheeks, the girl yelled, "No, we can't leave her like this!"

John lifted Jessica's shoulders and head. "Get her legs."

Stumbling through debris, they carried Jessica's body to the wash-house. They covered her with a blanket and another aftershock rattled the room. They ran into the street, stood in the semidarkness until the shock subsided. Firemen were battling the flames that flared in many of the buildings. The horse team that pulled one of the fire engines snorted and stamped as firemen dragged hoses and shouted instructions.

They sat on a slab of stone at the edge of Meeting Street. Before the quake had done its raging work, the stone had been part of the hospital's entryway arch. Now it was just a big piece of rubble.

Elbows on knees, the girl sobbed. Her back heaved. In a few minutes, the sobs turned into occasional jerks in her breath.

She stared at the ground. Her cheeks were streaked beneath her eyes where tears had washed the dust.

John leaned toward her, pulling a handkerchief from his pocket. "Is it okay if I get some of that off you?" She nodded. He shook the handkerchief, she closed her eyes and he wiped carefully around them. "There, that's better."

She opened her eyes. "Well thanks. Y'know, mine isn't the only face could use washing."

"I'll get to it, maybe when we can get some water. But y'know, I'd really like to call you something other than Miss."

"I'm Sherry. Sherry Ainslee. You?"

"John Archer."

Sherry Ainslee looked at John carefully. Her eyebrows lowered in a squint, her brow wrinkled. That name was in her memory. Somewhere, sometime in the past.

For three hours they worked together, searching the hospital for those still living, helping or carrying them to the treatment rooms, washing and binding wounds. They were exhausted when, at two in the morning, another aftershock rocked the building. They moved to the middle of the street. It was filled with people, some sitting on the street, some in makeshift shelters.

John said, "I guess this is the place to be, certainly isn't safe in a building. I'm gonna get some stuff from my room, I'll be right back."

He walked to the boarding house, climbed the wobbly stairs to his second-floor room. Its door hung askew on one hinge. His desk was covered with plaster and his books were scattered on the floor. His lamp lay on its side in the debris. He picked it up and dragged his mattress and some blankets down the stairs into the street. Using broken timbers for support, they rigged a tent of sorts above the mattress.

John said, "Where's your room, Sherry?"

"It's in the dormitory, about a block from here."

"Is it safe to go in?"

"I think so, at least if it hasn't fallen down worse than when I got out."

They walked to the dorm. Its second floor had collapsed onto the first. The first-floor room she'd shared with Jessica was filled with debris, mainly plaster and plaster lath. As John wrenched a piece of lath off the bed, it snapped and flew back at his head. The sharp end scraped him below his right eye, gouging a streak in his cheek.

"John, are you all right?" Sherry held a lamp close to his face. "That looks nasty."

"I don't think it's deep, it really doesn't hurt much."

They pulled blankets, a bag of clothing and her mattress from beneath the rubble and carried them to the tent. They shook the bedding and beat it with their fists, dislodging clouds of plaster dust in the lamplight, and laid the mattress alongside his.

"Okay, now let me look at that cut." She held the lamp close. "You're right, it's not deep. But it needs to be cleaned. I need some water."

A voice came from a shelter behind them. "I've got some."

John turned, held up his lamp. "Moses! Oh, I'm so glad you're all right."

Moses Camplin, the only negro student in his class, carried a small bucket of water to their tent. "We got water to use workin' in the ER, and I figured some might come in handy over the night. At least to drink, but we can spare some to clean you up."

"Moses, this is Sherry, she's in the nursing school, we been workin' together."

Sherry took a pair of underpants from her bag of clothes, ripped them in half and poured water over the rag. "Good to meet you, Moses."

She cleaned the blood around John's cut and washed the worst of the grime from his face. Moses had wiped his face, but streaks of plaster dust still lay on his brown skin. When Sherry finished cleaning John's face she moved to him.

"You got most of it off, but there are places that look like a kid was playin' on a blackboard." They grinned. She wiped at the streaks as they traded the horrible stories of the evening.

Moses had been working with the quake's casualties since it hit. At 4 am another aftershock jostled their mattresses. Ten minutes later, exhausted, they all fell asleep.

September 2, 1886

> The three students follow an undertaker's wagon through ruined streets to a graveyard at the edge of the city. John and Moses stand alongside Sherry, John's arm over her shaking shoulders, as Jessica is buried.

That night they sat on their mattresses at the Meeting Street encampment by lanternlight, surrounded by Charleston's wrecked buildings. Moses had retrieved a bottle of rum and some tin cups from a battered supply cabinet in the Roper wreckage. He poured a little into their three cups.

"Medical therapy, y'know. Good for stress, hysteria, aches and pains, most anything else that ails ya."

John raised his cup. "Glad you found some medicine, Moses. I need it."

Sherry said, "We all need it. This sure isn't what I pictured school would be. Seems like we're taking the final exam before we hardly got started."

Moses nodded. "That's for sure. I splinted two broken arms and a broken leg today. Dr. Michel showed me what to do for the first one, but I was on my own after that."

Another aftershock shook the street. The lantern flared and the poles supporting the makeshift tent trembled. One slid sideways.

John straightened the crooked pole. "Nobody said we'd be learning medicine in a war zone. Thank god there hasn't been anything like that first day."

Moses nodded. "Amen to that."

Sherry raised her cup. "Moses, pour just a little more. For Jessica."

With their cups filled, they touched them together.

"To lovely Jessica, graduated in a way we'd never have imagined." Sherry said. "God, I miss her."

"To lovely Jessica."

Sherry broke the silence. "John, how on earth did you end up here in Charleston. I mean, Moses and I are from here, but you're a long way from Maryland."

He related the story. How the war had brought his father from Maryland to Carolina, the farm in Winnsboro, selling it to Josh Ranson. Farming with his father and grandparents in Buckeystown, working cotton with Josh for two years, then his decision to leave farming and study medicine.

But not all the story. Not why they'd left Winnsboro. Not his mother's color.

Moses poured them another cup. They sat and talked half an hour, when the rum and exhaustion sent them to their mattresses.

> The weeks that follow are filled with work, starting in early morning, going till well after dark. And filled with medical learning, not dry lectures and blackboards, but the doctors from the college working with them to help quake-damaged bodies and minds. With both city hospitals ruined, patients are

treated at the former U.S. Marine Hospital, which had been abandoned during the war. Built of wood, the hospital and its associated barracks were spared the major damage suffered by the more rigid brick buildings. Aftershocks continue at erratic intervals, but become less frequent and less violent as the days pass. Every evening the students return to their encampment on Meeting Street and sit together on their mattresses by lamplight.

Sipping and talking had become an evening ritual for the three.

John held out his cup: "God, am I exhausted. Moses, could you splash a little more of that rum in here?"

Moses replenished their cups. "So, what'd you deal with today?"

Sherry answered, "Mostly it was the usual, cuts, bruises, broken bones. But there were some strange ones. We had one woman come in with no hair. It'd started falling out in clumps out the day after the quake, by the end of the week she was completely bald. Doctor Pelzer diagnosed 'paralysis of the scalp caused by fright.'"

John grinned. "That's a new one to me, I didn't know a scalp could be paralyzed."

Moses said, "Guess that's why we're in med school, learn new stuff. And this quake sure is showing how the mind can affect the body. One of the profs told me he'd seen in today's paper that three women were frightened to death that night."

"Can somebody actually be frightened to death?" Sherry asked.

John shook his head. "Who knows. If it's true it means less work for us."

Moses nodded. "And more for the undertakers. That prof said the paper reported the quake killed twenty-seven people."

"And that number's sure going up. Folks are dying from infection of the injuries they got that night. We lost three today." John said.

Sherry said, "Wouldn't be surprised if we lose more from folks falling down or stepping in front of wagons. The bars are absolutely full, drunks all over the place. And the drug stores are running out of laudanum and the other sedatives."

John sipped his rum. "Talkin' about drug stores, the hospital was totally out of laudanum, so I stopped in the one on George Street this morning to get some. The manager told me his clerk Anthony disappeared the day of the quake. He got hold of Anthony's father a couple of days later, tryin' to get him back to work. The father said he was probably gone for good. When the quake happened, Anthony'd just started walking, didn't stop till he got to Yemassee, y'know that's a fifty mile walk, and sent a postcard home saying he couldn't come back."

"That's some walkin' fool," Moses said. He shook his head. "Think I'm done with rum for tonight, gonna sack out. It sure is gettin' cold, I hope the college figgers a way to get us outta the street soon. I haven't got any more blankets to cover up with. Goodnight."

"Goodnight Moses."

John turned out the lantern and lay down on his mattress alongside Sherry. They lay close, facing each other.

"So, tell me more. Who are you, John Archer? Your folks had a farm near Winnsboro, my home's maybe twenty miles north of there, we were almost neighbors."

"Yeah, I guess we were, but that was a long time ago. We moved to Maryland when I was just a baby."

"But you moved back, and you grew cotton."

"Yup, did it for two years. That was enough for me. I guess I just needed time to figure out what I wanted to do with my life, and farming—cotton or whatever—just wasn't it."

"You decided medicine was?"

"Yup. How about you, how'd you get here?"

"Well, a little bit like you. There's hardly any jobs around Winnsboro but farmin', so when I got outta high school I went up to Rock Hill, worked at store called Ivy and Fewell for awhile."

"What were you doin'?"

"I, sir, was a seamstress in the millinery department working for Miss Waller, making and modifying dresses."

"Ah, you can sew!"

"Darn right I can."

"So why aren't you workin' for Miss Waller anymore, miss seamstress?"

"Well, maybe it's like you and cotton. Sewin's a way to make a living, but that's about all. I guess if you're nuts about clothes you really get into it, but I'm not. Some gals seem to feel like what they're wearin' shows what they are inside. I never did feel that way."

"How did you feel?"

"I guess a lot like you. I don't think there's any better work than helping to heal folks. I knew about this medical school and wrote to see if I could get in."

"A woman doctor, huh. What'd they say?"

"You know what they said. That's why I'm in nursing school."

"Well, I'm sorry you're not in the med school, but I'm sure glad you're here with me tonight."

She reached to his mattress, put her hand on his.

A cotton farmer turned doctor, that's some career change. Born here, moved north, now he's back here. But there sure is somethin' familiar about his name. Well, maybe I'll find out sometime. Must be a month now we

94

been sleeping alongside each other
here, and I sure do like what I'm seein'
in him. I sure do.

They fell asleep holding hands.

April 30, 1887

A letter for Sherry arrives at the Marine Hospital. Her parents are worried about her.

...the earthquake wasn't too bad here,
but everything we've been reading says
it was awful in Charleston. Are you all
right? I guess someone would've told us
if you were bad injured, or God forbid,
dead, but please, please write, let us
know how you're doing.

Sherry wrote back immediately, starting with a heartfelt apology for not being in touch.

...I'm so, so sorry, it just got so frantic
here dealing with all the earthquake
injuries I forgot to write you. I'm fine, just
fine, and learning lots. The trains are
really running yet, the tracks are all torn
up, but as soon as I can I'll come visit.

It was two months before the trains were able to resume any kind of regular schedule. Sherry sent her parents a letter telling them when she'd be arriving.

Photo Courtesy of the University of South Carolina

In the early morning November chill, she and John walked north through Charleston's ruins. Roof beams from a factory lay angled into the road. Rooms in apartments gaped open, their exterior walls rubble in the street. The base of a cross protruded from the bricks that had once been a church's steeple. The railroad station's roof had collapsed onto the tracks, so trains now stopped two miles north of the city. It was a long walk.

John said, "Did you hear, we can finally get out of the damn street. The college put up a notice there's rooms in the old Marine barracks we can rent, finally get a real roof over our heads."

"Sounds good to me. It's gettin' cold, and I'm tired of living out there."

"Actually, I rented a room already. It's not great, but it's big enough for two people. Whaddya think?"

She smiled. "Hmm. Big enough for two people, huh? You got a brother or somethin'?"

"No, I don't have a brother. I think you know what I'm thinkin'."

"Yeah, I guess I do."

"Thought you would. And there's something I want you to think about while you're gone. Don't have to answer now, but when you get back."

"Mmm. Sounds like somethin' more important than buyin' a new pair of shoes."

"It is. It's whether you'll marry me."

"Marry you, huh? What makes you think I'll marry you, mister? The fact we been sleepin' alongside each other for months?"

"Yeah, guess that's got somethin' to do with it. And I guess what's happened is I've fallen in love with you. And I get the feelin' I'm not the only one doin' that."

"She grinned at him."You get that feeling, huh? Even feeling that I just might say yes?"

"Yeah, I think you just might. But don't give me an answer now, think on it while you're off with your folks, let me know when you come back."

"Okay. When I get back."

They kissed goodbye and she got into the northbound train.

"I'll be back as soon as I can. I'll miss you."

"You know I'll miss you. Not more than a week, right?"

"Right. And I'll have an answer for you. For us."

The train whistle blew twice. The engine's pistons spewed steam, threw their power on the locomotive's steel wheels. They skidded, squealing, then grabbed the track. The train lurched forward, car couplers clanking. Looking out the window, Sherry waved as a cloud of steam enveloped John. He waved back until the train was out of sight, turned and started back into the city. The farther he walked, the worse he felt.

Why hadn't he told her? Was their love really
dependent on what color his mother's skin was?
Could that be? Why should it be, love is love

dammit! But sooner or later she'd know. Even if
they never visited his folks in Maryland and they
never came here, she'd know. She'd find out. And
what color would their babies be? He had to tell
her. Why hadn't he told her, dammit? And what
would she say?

The train steamed north through Branchville and Orangeburg. South of Orangeburg an engine lay on its side by the tracks, hurled by the force of the quake. They came to a halt twice, the engineer descending from the cab to examine the rails ahead. They passed track crews repairing damage, once stopped for half an hour as a rail was replaced. At Columbia Sherry changed to a smaller train and finally, as the sun set over the Winnsboro station, there were her parents.

"Sherry, Sherry!" Martha hugged her joyously as she stepped from the car. "Oh, so good to see you! Are you alright?"

"Yes mom, yes, I'm fine, I'm just fine."

Homer wrapped his arms around Sherry as soon as his wife released her. "Ah my little girl, my not-so-little girl. Thank God you're home."

He picked up her suitcase and they walked to the cart, Martha peppering Sherry with questions, hardly waiting for an answer. All three jammed onto the seat, Homer slapped the reins over the horse's back and they headed home.

As the wagon stopped in front of the house, Sherry's 15-year-old sister Harriet rushed through the door and threw her arms around Sherry. "So, so glad you're home, sis. I wanna hear all your stories!"

After supper they sat in the kitchen talking. They hadn't all been together since Christmas, nine long months. So much, so much to say. School, it was going fine she assured them. The earthquake, yes it was horrible. She described the damage and the long hours of work. Finding her roommate dead in the collapsed hospital. Living on the street.

Harriet asked, "You live on the street! Why?"

98

"It was the only safe place after the quake. It just wasn't safe to be in a building because of the aftershocks, and anyhow, my room was wrecked. But the aftershocks are less violent now, folks are moving back into buildings. John and I are planning to share an apartment."

Martha raised her eyebrows. "John. Who's John?"

"We've been living under the same tent roof on the street since the quake. And we've been working together almost constantly. I don't know what I would've done without him."

"Sounds like you got more than just professional interest in this fella."

"Okay, has this John got a last name?" Martha asked.

"Archer. John Archer."

Homer leaned back in his chair, closed his eyes. "Where's John Archer from?"

"He's from Maryland, a town called Buckeystown."

"Did he always live there?"

"No, his family used to have a farm down near here."

Martha nodded. "The Archers. The Archers Josh Ranson brought here when he was taking them up to Rock Hill. Those Archers."

Sherry frowned. "Whaddya mean 'those Archers'? What's wrong with 'those Archers'?"

"Did you know his mother's colored?"

"What?"

"She's a nigra. She's as brown as...as brown as my belt." Homer said.

"That can't be, he's just as white as you or me!"

Half an hour later Martha knocked on the door of the bedroom Harriet and Sherry were sharing. Sherry, sitting on the bed, stared out the window. Martha could tell she'd been crying. She sat on the bed alongside her, took her hand.

99

"So he didn't tell you?"

Sherry shook her head.

"He should have. It's important."

"I know. I know."

"What are you goin' to do?"

"I don't know. I don't know."

Two days later a message came for John at the Marine Hospital, Sherry would be returning on the train the next day. He got to the makeshift station north of Charleston several hours before the train was supposed to arrive. He paced the gravel along the tracks, sat on a beam extending from a pile of wreckage, then paced, then sat, searching for what he could say.

Why didn't I tell her? Why, dammit? What should I say now? And what will she say?

Finally the train whistle sounded in the distance, the engine's smoke rolled above the trees to the north. He stood rigid as the engine steamed past and the cars squealed to a stop. His eyes strained for her as passengers descended. Carrying her suitcase, there she was. She was smiling, damn, he hoped that was a good sign.

He ran to her, they hugged in silence. He stepped back, held up a hand.

"Wait, wait. I know I told you I wanted an answer about getting married as soon as you got back. But there's something important I've gotta tell you first."

"Important?"

"Very important."

"I know. My folks told me. I don't care. I want to marry you."

****

The Medical College building was so badly damaged it couldn't be used for more than a year, but classes resumed two months after the quake in the Marine Hospital. John and Sherry moved into a room in

100

one of hospital barracks. He'd rented the room in his name, not mentioning her, but figured if he had a guest, that was his business.

And finally, finally they had a bed, a real bed with sheets and pillows, in a private place. A bed where, for the first time, they made love. Her body was long, strong, supple, small-breasted. Both virgins, they had much to learn about sex, and were thrilled with every lesson.

Days were hard and long, filled with classes and patients dealing with injuries from the earthquake, but every night their love's reward awaited. It was common that much of their supper—usually bread and cheese bought at a roadside stand—still sat on the beside table when they woke in the morning.

John: "God, this stuff's stale."

"Are you complaining?"

"A little."

"Look at it this way, breakfast's ready. You just gotta chew a bit harder."

June 4, 1887

Sherry and John stand before the preacher at Wentworth Street Protestant Church in Charleston and say the words "I do." They're marrying there instead of Winnsboro for a certain type of privacy. Folks in Winnsboro would likely remember John's mother was colored. In Charleston, that was unlikely.

Sherry's parents were there, but not John's. Carolyn's feelings about Carolina hadn't changed much despite the passing years. She hadn't wanted to return there when Josh got married, and she still didn't. Frank had decided he wouldn't leave Carolyn alone. They sent the kids a loving letter and an invitation, almost a demand, that they come to Maryland for a visit. They'd have a second celebration of the marriage there.

Josh and Corinne Ranson were there, Josh serving as John's best man. Sherry's sister Harriet, now a lovely 16-year-old, was the bridesmaid. Moses was there too. He and John had talked about him being best man or a groom in the wedding, but decided that would be too much of a challenge to Carolina society.

> As a married couple, John and Sherry are entitled to better quarters at the Marine Hospital barracks. They move into a small apartment with a kitchen, a sitting room and a bedroom. In the Spring of 1887 repairs to the Medical College are completed and classes resume there. Sherry graduates from nursing school at the end of 1887, John from medical school in June of 1888.

When they left Charleston, wreckage from the earthquake littered some city lots, but much had been repaired and rebuilt. They said goodbye to professors and fellow students, and Moses accompanied them to the now-rebuilt train station.

Once again, the Ainslees met them at the Winnsboro station. They'd not been together since the wedding a year ago and the reunion was joyous. They talked nonstop all the way to the farm, the men on the wagon's seat, Martha, Sherry and Harriet on mattresses in the wagon's bed.

In the morning they sat around the breakfast table. Carolina's economy had improved since the end of the war, and breakfast was substantial: bacon, eggs, toast and hot coffee. Real coffee, not the roasted acorns that had substituted during the war and for years afterwards.

Homer said, "So, you're planning on practicing medicine in Rock Hill? Why not here, we've gotta go clear to Columbia if we need a doctor?"

"Well, it's mostly a matter of size. Rock Hill's got probably five times as many folks as Winnsboro, and it's growing really fast. They're a railroad junction, coupla lines, and they're gettin' pretty big into textiles. They just got a steam-powered cotton mill. If that works out Carolina'll be able to make its own cloth instead of shipping all our cotton somewhere else to get it done."

"All comes down to numbers, huh?"

"Well, a doctor needs numbers. If you haven't got many people, you're not gonna have many sick people, right?"

Martha spoke. "Well, we sure wish you'd figger out a way to stay here."

Sherry replied. "Mom, it's only thirty miles or so, and there's a train goes right there. We'll be able to visit plenty, much easier than when we were clear down in Charleston."

Harriet agreed. "Yeah, Mom, they won't be so far away. It'll be fun to visit, we can even go up to Charlotte from there! I mean Winnsboro's okay, but it can get pretty boring. Charlotte's got all sorts of stores, and I hear sometimes they have the Cole Brothers circus. "

Homer answered, "Boring, huh. We're boring?"

"Oh, dad, no you're not boring. But it'd be exciting to go to the city once in awhile. I could use a break from gutting chickens and washing poop off eggs. And there'll be guys there. Thanks to that darn war there's hardly any left here."

In bed that evening, John turned to Sherry. "I was really worried about how your folks were gonna take finding out my mother's colored, but it seems like it's pretty much okay. Or if it's not, they're hiding it pretty good."

"I talked some with mom after supper, and it's pretty much okay. They're not like some of the folks down here, they've even got a coupla colored families they consider friends."

"That's good to hear."

103

"I think more than anything they're concerned about what its effect is gonna be on us."

The next day Homer took John to the train station, headed for Rock Hill. Two weeks later he'd rented an office and a big house at the edge of the city. Sherry joined him, and the Rock Hill Herald announced they were in business.

John R. Archer, M.D.
(Office over J.J. Haggins & Co drug store)
MAIN STREET
ROCK HILL, S. CAROLINA
Will practice in City and County

Most of the half-dozen doctors in Rock Hill avoided colored patients, but John and Sherry did not, so much of their initial clientele was impoverished ex-slaves. As a result they didn't prosper financially in a hurry. However, often paid in eggs, vegetables, and hams, they were in no danger of malnutrition.

Boosted by its status as a railroad junction, Rock Hill blossomed, its population approaching 2000. Four cotton mills opened. New folks moved in. Local landowners sold them lots, builders built them houses. A range of new businesses opened and prospered. Money flowed.

One cool Fall afternoon as 1890 moved toward winter. Josephine Smolinski stood, arms folded, on her house's front steps, admiring the street's new addition. Four of her girls stood behind her.

"Sure looks good, don't it ladies!"

They were admiring the new concrete sidewalk, which Josephine's thriving business had paid for.

Sally nodded, "Sure does, Josephine. It's class!. And maybe the guys won't bring so damn much mud in the house now."

Rock Hill's first poured sidewalk was purchased by The Bordello, the town's busy whorehouse.

Shortly after The Bordello's contribution to Rock Hill, its streets shone at night. A dynamo at the Black Street power station, driven by an 80-horsepower engine, sent electricity through the town's newly installed wires, lighting sixty streetlamps and 200 commercial lights.

The Archer's practice, which included some of the Bordello's girls, also steadily grew, and its expertise became well-known. At the beginning of 1890, Moses Camplin had joined the practice, making it the only mixed-race medical practice in the city. But the partnership was tolerated. The value of good medicine insulated them from some of the prejudice that affected most relationships between Black and White.

But not all of it.

The Pussy Parade

Susan helped Sally Mazzaschi up the Archer's steps and held the door open for her. Sally, a tiny blonde, was supporting her swollen right forearm with her left hand.

Sherry saw them come through the door. "What happened, Sally?"

"One of the guys got mad cause I wouldn't do something he wanted, and he grabbed my arm and bent it way back. It hurts somethin' awful!"

Sherry opened the door to the examination room. "Well, come in, sit on the exam table there, and the doctor will be right in."

Sally's eyes opened wide when Moses Camplin came in.

"Where's Doctor Archer? I thought I'd be seeing Doctor Archer!"

"Well, he's out on a house call right now."

105

"When will he be back?"

"Well, it's hard to say. He's with a woman having a baby, and you never know how long that will take."

"My arm really hurts!"

"Do you want me to look at it?"

There was a moment of silence. "I guess."

Moses examined the arm. "It looks like one of the bones is broken, but as far as I can tell it's not displaced. It should heal up fine, but you're not going to be able to use it for awhile. Sherry, can you get me the leather we use for splinting?"

Moses cut a sleeve from the leather and wrapped Sally's forearm.

"This will hold the bone so it can heal properly. Come back tomorrow, in the meantime don't use this arm for anything."

Sally and Susan returned the next day, and the day after that. By the second day, the swelling had subsided, and Moses replaced the leather sleeve with a splint fashioned from willow.

"It's looking good. You keep resting this arm, don't use it for anything, and come back next week."

They started back to the Bordello. Sally said, "Well, that asshole Butch sure put a hurtin' on my arm, I dunno when I'm gonna be able to work again."

"I don't hardly think you'll miss a beat. Josephine banned Butch from the place, so you won't be seein' him again. And she knows what the guys who come in are like, she'll make sure you don't get any more rough customers." She giggled, "Anyhow, it's not like they come in for your arm!"

"Yeah, you're right. My pussy ain't hurt a bit."

"There ya go. You'll get through it okay, and it looks like this doc will have you healed up pretty quick. Seems to know what he's doin'"

"Well, I had my doubts when I saw he's a nigger, but seems like he's an okay doctor."

106

They passed two little boys playing on the sidewalk. One of them, maybe four years old, was spinning a top.

Susan reached down and ruffled the boy's hair. "Pretty cute, ain't he."

"Yeah, he is."

They approached the Bordello.

"You ever think about havin' kids?" Susan said.

"Yeah, I do. A lot. But somehow I gotta get outta this place. Sometimes I wonder how the hell I got here anyhow."

"I know how I did. It's a way I can count on to make some money, to eat."

"Yeah, guess it was the same for me, but I sure get tired of it sometimes."

"Me too. I keep hopin' one of these days Mister Right will come along, fall in love, and get me outta here. But till that happens, if I wanna keep eatin' good and havin' nice clothes, I gotta keep lettin' 'em parade through my pussy."

"A parade, huh?"

"Yeah, wavin' their batons and blowin' their damn horns."

Susan held the Bordello's door open for Sally. Josephine and one of the girls at a table playing checkers.

"What's the news on your arm?" said Josephine.

"The doc says it's healin' up okay."

"Good. I'm sorry it happened and I'm doin' everything I can to make sure it don't happen again. To you, to any of the girls. You ready for some checkers?"

"Sure. Only need one hand for that."

"You're up soon as we finish this game. I've got her pretty well whipped, so it won't be long."

Soon after moving to Rock Hill, Sherry got pregnant, but suffered a miscarriage two months into the pregnancy. The sequence repeated itself two years later. Sid Beckett, her doctor, said she should avoid getting pregnant, it was too risky to her health. But he said pregnancy was unlikely, she'd had some changes in her private parts.

June James

Some said June James was the prettiest woman in York County, or at least she had been. A statuesque, buxom blonde, she was tall, close to six feet. She'd grown up on a small farm south of Rock Hill with her widowed aunt. Twenty-five years old, like so many Southern girls after the war, she was well into the status of spinster. Shy and quiet, a habitual reader, she loved novels and kept a diary full of her thoughts and dreams, which included finding a good man. With a quarter of Carolina's white men dead and another quarter disabled, pickings were slim.

Her diary entry from September 1, 1889.
Thinking about babies today. Again. Will I ever have one? I so want one so badly. But where's the man who'll give me one? Seems like all the men here are already married or just aren't interested in getting that way. I talked to Arthur Torrington awhile at the Fair last month and I thought for awhile he might ask me out, but he hasn't. And none of the men at church pay much attention, except old Mister MacReady. I guess he's okay, he's got a good job and everyone in town seems to know him. But we'd make a pretty strange couple, he's so much shorter than me. And he sure ain't good-looking.

Obadiah

Of Ebenezer Presbyterian Church's forty-some congregation, Obadiah MacReady was one of only seven men. Four or five inches shorter than June, he wore his black hair slicked across his head to cover its burgeoning bald spot. He was thirty years June's senior, and walked with a limp, the result of a Union bullet through his leg when his unit retreated from Columbia. The wound had healed but the scar remained. With his fellow RedShirts, he'd cheered for Wade Hampton at his Rock Hill rallies.

He described June to Ben Melson, the town's deputy sheriff, as they sipped whiskey in the Bordello's comfortable front room.

"Yeah, she's a looker, Ben, and what a body! I'd sure love to feel those long legs she got!"

"Better'n sweet Sally?"

"Well, just as good."

"That's sayin' somethin'. Maybe you oughta get to know her better."

"You know I'm gonna do that."

Six months later Obadiah MacReady and June were married at the Ebenezer Presbyterian Church.

December 18, 1890

June had been a patient of the Archer practice for nearly two years when Sherry examined her one chilly day. The women knew each other, not just from their contact in the office. Though growing, Rock Hill was still small enough that most everybody knew everybody, seeing neighbors at church, the general store, the post office, the cobbler.

June's right eye was blackened, swollen almost shut.

"Well, that doesn't look nice. How did it happen?"

June frowned, looked up at the ceiling.

"It's almost the same as last time you were here, just the other eye. You bumped into a door frame again?"

Tears burst down June's cheeks. Her words came between sobs.

"It was Obadiah!"

"And last time, was that really him too?"

109

She nodded.

"Are you hurt anywhere else?"

"Yeah, it really hurts to sit."

"Let me see."

She lay stomach-down on the table and raised her long skirt. The backs of her thighs were covered with bruises.

"So it hurts where you sit too?"

"Yes. A lot."

"Can I see?"

She slid her underpants down. Bruises striped her buttocks. Some terminated with partly healed punctures.

"That looks pretty awful. What did he hit you with?"

"His belt."

"You can sit up."

June stood, pulled her skirt back down.

Sherry asked, "Why did he hit you?"

"I don't know. Sometimes he comes home drunk, mad about something or other. It's my cooking or how I look, anything. When he's that way it seems like everything about me is wrong. And he found my diary and read through it."

"Was there something in it that set him off?"

"Well, I do write stuff in there that I feel. It's supposed to be just for me, but he found it in the clothing drawer where I keep it, and he read it. I guess he didn't like some of it, maybe some of the stuff I wrote about him. And about other men."

"Have you told anyone else about this?"

"No. Who could I tell?"

"Your minister?"

"I did, but he wasn't any help. He seems to feel a wife's duty includes this kinda stuff."

"How about the sheriff, if you talked to him he could talk to Obadiah."

"Gosh, no. They're friends, it'd just make it worse."

110

Sherry frowned, crossed the room and sat in a chair, looking down.

"Have you ever thought about maybe just leaving him? Just go away, make a new start somewhere else. I know it'd be hard, but if he keeps doing this you could get really hurt."

"I have thought about about leaving."

"Where would you go?"

She grimaced. "I don't want to talk about it."

Lying in bed that evening, Sherry told John about the MacReadys.

"I'd heard things weren't good in that marriage, but I didn't realize how bad. So Obadiah's been beating her?" John asked.

"Yes. I thought maybe if she told the sheriff he could talk to Obadiah, but she says that's an awful idea. They're friends, both regulars at the Bordello"

"I guess she's right." He shook his head. "She's in a tough situation."

"It's sad. She's a sweet girl."

They lay in silence. John sighed, turned his head, eyes played over her face. He stroked her cheek, her neck, her breast.

"You are so beautiful, my love, so beautiful."

Two months later, the MacReady's relationship plays out tragically. The Charlotte paper reports it in two stories, one before, one after the lynching. The paper's inconsistency is spectacular, reversing the "negro brute's" name from one story to the second, and assuming his guilt without a trial. Significantly, the second story—in contrast to the first—omits him claiming he was sent there by a man with whom Mrs.

111

MacReady planned to run away.

Charlotte Clarion, March 15, 1891

The negro brute Fletcher Magruder, who outraged the person of Mrs. Obediah MacReady, on Sunday night last, says that he was sent there by a man, with whom Mrs. MacReady had made arrangements to elope, and that not getting off, and for fear of being caught, brought this charge against him. His story is not given any credence whatever. The people are greatly excited over the affair and Fletcher will probably be lynched immediately upon Capt. MacReady's return to Rock Hill.

Charlotte Clarion, March 17, 1891
MAGRUDER FLETCHER LYNCHED.

A Party of Masked Men Take him from Prison — His Body Shockingly Mutilated

The negro Magruder Fletcher, who criminally assaulted Mrs. Obadiah MacReady several days ago, was lynched about 3 o'clock a.m. today by a party of about seventy-five men. Jailer Samuel Melson was aroused about 1 o'clock by a party of masked men who demanded the keys of the jail. Melson refused to give them up. He was told that if he did not his house would be burned, but he still refused. Deputy

Sheriff Benjamin L. Melson, who had been aroused by the commotion, came to the scene and told the jailer he had better hand over the keys which he did. The lynchers went to the cell of Fletcher and told him he was wanted. He was at once released and was carried out. He made no demurrer whatever. The doors of the jail were fastened by the lynchers and the keys turned over to the jailer. The negro was then hurried off and hung to a limb of a pine tree on the edge of the road about one and a half miles from here. He was cut down at about nine o'clock by Magistrate Higgins and a coroner's inquest was held. The verdict was rendered that Fletcher came to his death by being strangled and shot by persons unknown to the jury. His neck was not broken. He was also shockingly mutilated. It is supposed that this was done prior to the hanging. Fletcher was a stout man of about twenty-five years of age and was very black. The public approves the lynching. Mrs. MacReady's husband came home yesterday. The lady is in a very precarious condition and is about crazed.

See Note at end of The Story

Such vigilante justice was common in rural areas of the country, and in this period South Carolina was no exception. Death of "suspects" by lynching far outnumbered death sentences imposed by a court trial. Early in his twenty-three years as a U.S. Senator, "Pitchfork" Ben Tillman, who'd personally executed Black legislator Simon Coker in 1876 in Hamburg, expressed his support for the practice and the oft-heard obsession with protecting the virtue of white women.

> *We of the South have never recognized the right of the negro to govern white men, and we never will. We have never believed him to be the equal of the white man, and we will not submit to his gratifying his lust on our wives and daughters without lynching him.*
>
> *I have three daughters but, so help me God, I had rather find either one of them killed by a tiger or a bear [and die a virgin] than to have her crawl to me and tell me the horrid story that she had been robbed of the jewel of her womanhood by a black fiend.*

Some years later, Pitchfork Ben addressed a RedShirt reunion in Anderson, South Carolina, and recounted the events of 1876, events for which he was indicted but never prosecuted:

> *The purpose of our visit to Hamburg was to strike terror, and the next morning ... the ghastly sight which met their gaze of seven dead negroes lying stark and stiff, certainly had its effect ... It was now after midnight, and the moon high in the heavens looked down peacefully on the deserted town and dead negroes, whose lives had been offered up as a sacrifice to the fanatical teachings and fiendish hate of those who sought to substitute the rule of the*

African for that of the Caucasian in South Carolina.

Support for lynching wasn't limited to politicians. The Vicksburg Evening Post printed a summary of a sermon delivered in New York by the Right Reverend Hugh Miller Thompson, Bishop of Mississippi. From that summary:

LYNCHING JUSTIFIED BY A BISHOP

"..in all the years I have lived in the South I have never known a doubtful lynching....The laws are slow, the jails are full, and the lawyers banded together to defeat justice, as they always are. The offense is a capital one all over the South, so the people save delay by simply resuming their natural sovereignty ...and hang the criminal."

July, 1903

John's medical practice, now Archer & Camplin MDs, continues to prosper. A second nurse, Regina Sandifer, has joined the practice. They continue to treat patients regardless of color, but their expertise has attracted patients of all economic status. John, now a respected citizen, is named to the Board of Directors of the local teacher training school, Winthrop Normal and Industrial College.

Early one morning, Sherry stood in front of the bathroom mirror examining her face. Are those wrinkles worse than last week, worse than last month? And her period's been erratic, she hasn't had a real one for two, maybe three months.

This can't be happening! I can't be getting menopause at 36, dammit! Can I?

She told John, went to see Sid Beckett.

"Congratulations, Sherry. You're pregnant. I didn't think it would happen, but it has."

"Oh my god, I can't believe it! Does it seem like a normal pregnancy?"

"As far as I can tell, yes. You're about two months pregnant. Given your history, it would be best if you take it easy for awhile."

John was overjoyed. "Okay Miz nurse, you're on light duty from now on. Regina will take over anything that requires heavy lifting. I mean lifting of any kind, got it? Doctor's orders!"

"Got it, doctor."

Della

February 13, 1904

For Sherry, three is the magic number. She follows the doctor's orders, and her pregnancy is uneventful. At four in the afternoon, Della Archer, 7 pounds 1 ounce, comes into the world. Her parents are overjoyed. And her skin is quite white.

Even before she could walk, the world fascinated Della. Not buildings and machines, but life. People, yes, but also the little lives. Birds, bugs, mice, snakes, all those things that flew and crawled and breathed out in the world. When she was four, Sherry found her lying belly-down on the kitchen floor, her face inches from a snake. Six inches long, black with a yellow band around its neck, it was waving its tongue at her. Della was waving hers back.

"What kind of snake is it, Mommy?"

"Well, I don't know honey. I know it's not dangerous. Maybe we can get a book that will tell us."

They put the snake in a mason jar with holes punched in the

116

top. Della kept it by her bed until Sherry convinced her it would starve if they didn't let it go. Sherry drew a color picture of it before they let it go in the backyard. When the mailman delivered the snake book Sherry'd ordered, the book said it was a ring-neck snake.

When she was five, Della and Charles, Moses' six-year-old son, found a dead possum in the backyard. Fascinated by its grin, its long pointy teeth, they called Sherry.

"Why does it have hair everywhere but its tail, Mom?"

"Well, that's just the way it is, love. God makes his animals however he wants, I guess. We should bury it, it'll smell bad soon."

They buried the possum by the garden. Della planted a cardboard marker on the grave. Peter Possum. Two weeks later she dug Peter up.

"Why did you dig him up, honey?"

"I just wanted to see what was happening to him."

"What was happening?"

"He was yucky."

One morning after breakfast Sherry was brushing Della's hair in the kitchen.

"Mommy, what were you and Daddy doing last night?"

"What do you mean, dear?"

"Well, I had a bad dream and I woke up, and I heard you and Daddy talking really loud. It wasn't really talking, it was like shouting, but not like you were scared. Were you mad at him, was he mad at you?"

Sherry rolled her eyes, brushed.

"Was something wrong, were you mad?"

"No honey, we weren't mad. We were happy."

"So you shouted because you were happy?"

"Yes. Sometimes when married people get really really happy they shout."

"I don't hear you or Daddy shout like that in the daytime."

"No, we don't."

"So why did you do it last night?"

Sherry kept brushing. "Well, when married people are all alone together and there's nothing they need to do, like brush hair or cook or clean, they just really enjoy paying good attention to each other."

"So that's 'paying good attention' shouting?"

"Yes."

"When I got up and came in your bedroom this morning, it looked like you didn't have your pajamas on, they were lying on the floor. Were you all naked in bed with Daddy?"

Sherry stopped brushing.

"Yes honey. Sometimes married people get naked in bed."

"Why?"

"Well, it feels good to hug someone you love when you don't have clothes on."

"Better than when you do?"

"It's good both ways."

Later that week, Sherry was again brushing Della's hair, after breakfast.

"You were right, Mommy."

"What was I right about?"

"It does feel good to hug someone you love without any clothes on."

Sherry stopped brushing. "What?"

"It does feel good, you're right."

Oh god, what have I done now? "What do you mean it does feel good, why are you saying that?"

"Well, I told Charles what you told me, and we both took our clothes off in the backyard yesterday and we pushed our tummies together, and it did feel good. His skin really felt good, all smooth. And it looked good, his all brown and mine just a little bit."

Sherry closed her eyes, sighed. "And what did you do then?"

118

"We put our clothes back on and went down to the creek."

Sherry resumed brushing. "Della, I want you to promise me you won't do that again."

"Not get naked with Charles?"

"That's right, not get naked with Charles. You forgot part of what I told you the other day, getting naked together is for after you get married."

"Why?"

"Well, it just is. There are things you do when you're a child and things you do when you're grown up. Boys and girls don't get naked together until they're older, until they're married."

"Why?"

Finished brushing, Sherry began braiding Della's hair into ponytails.

"Think of it like this. Do you remember when Shawn down the street got hurt by his daddy's plowhorse and had that cast on his leg for so long?"

"Yes."

"Well, he wasn't supposed to, but he'd opened the stall door and got that horse out. I guess he thought he'd ride him or something, I don't know. He was trying to put a bridle or a halter on the horse and it reared up, maybe something spooked it. When it came down one of its hoofs landed on Shawn's foot and broke it."

"Was he naked?"

Sherry suppressed a giggle. "No honey, he wasn't. It didn't matter whether he had clothes on or not, he was just too small to handle that horse. There are some things you don't do until you're grown up."

"Like getting naked together?"

"Like getting naked together."

That night Sherry lay in bed with John and told him the story.

John grinned. "That girl's somethin' else. Guess she's starting to grow up, huh?"

"She's starting. I just have to be careful not to say things that rush her. And we need to be quieter when we're lovin'."

"That would be a shame. Maybe we should just check her room first, make sure she's sound asleep. Maybe put a towel over that gap under the bedroom door.

"Why don't you go check her? And when you come back, get a towel."

Sherry shook her head, grinned. "And get naked?"

"I think you got the idea."

Charles and Della were playmates long after their naked adventure. He loved the outdoors as much as Della did, but wasn't as content just watching the animals. When they were nine he showed her his slingshot.

"You put a rock in this pouch here and pull the rubber bands like this."

He pulled them back and whoosh, the rock flew out. They lined empty tin cans up on a bench by the garden and took turns trying to hit them. Della loved it, even hit some of the cans.

When she got back home she burst through the kitchen door "Mom, mom, I want a slingshot!"

"A slingshot. What for?"

"It's fun."

"Well, we'll see. We'll talk to dad about it."
****
On Christmas morning that year a wooden slingshot protruded from the top of Della's stocking. She and Charles spent much of that afternoon killing cans in his garden. A week later they came into Sherry's kitchen with two squirrels.

"Look Mom, look! Can we have them for supper?"

"Well, they've gotta be skinned and cleaned first, you can't cook them like that. Let's see what your dad says when he gets home."

She wrapped the squirrels in paper and put them in the icebox. When John got home, after supper he showed Della how to skin and clean the squirrels. The next evening,Sherry and Della prepared supper together, cutting up the squirrels, potatoes and carrots. The family pronounced the squirrel stew excellent.

A week later, Charles and Della brought four squirrels home, and the Archers and Camplins shared the supper stew.

By the time Della was fourteen her room was a little biology museum. There were snakes and frogs in pickling jars on her shelves alongside half a dozen turtle shells and a possum skull. A red rat snake inhabited one aquarium alongside another holding mice to feed it. A preying mantis egg case hung from a locust branch. It was ragged, riddled with holes where one day the young mantises had eaten their way out of the case. That day the ceiling of the room had been speckled with tiny mantises looking for their first meal.

With the medical practice booming, John bought a Model T Ford, one of the first in town. It was far better than horseback to reach his patients and, when the weather was good, the family often drove to the South Mountains in North Carolina. They took a tent and spent long weekends hiking in the mountains.

They also drove the Ford up to Maryland each summer to visit Frank and Carolyn. Bothered with chest pains and arthritis, probably the result of months in wet trenches during the war, Frank wasn't the vigorous man he'd been. No longer up to farming, he'd rented his fields to Allen McAllister.

July 7, 1919
The telephone rang in the Archer house, Della answered. It was Carolyn.

"Hi Grandma, it's good to hear your voice."

"Hi sweetie, it's good to hear yours too. How are things in Rock Hill?"

121

"Just fine, school's out, I'm enjoying being outside and stuff. How are you and Granpa?"

There was a long pause. Della heard a sob.

"That's why I'm calling. Granpa died last night."

"Oh! Oh no, oh no!"

Carolyn, now obviously sobbing, "Is your mom or dad there?"

The next morning the Archers pulled up at the Buckeystown farmhouse in a drizzling rain. Dressed in black, Carolyn was on the porch with Darlene McAllister and Isabel. Sherry and Della hugged her, then John did. She leaned against him, sobbing.

"Mom, mom, it's gonna be alright."

"I don't know that anything will be alright ever again."

She clung to him, tears dripping on his shoulder.

John: "I know, I know. But you still have people who love you. We love you. Very very much."

"But Frank, he's gone. He's gone!"

He hugged her tight. "He'll always be with us. We can't hold him with our arms, but we can hold him in our hearts. And in our memories. They'll always be there. Always. As long as memories last."

Sherry and Della threw their arms around Carolyn and her son. Arms crossed in front of her, Darlene stood apart from the hugging family until Carolyn looked to her. Tear-blurred eyes drew her in. She spread her arms joined the hug.

Shortly after noon, the Archer's buggy rattled up Buckeystown Pike toward the Frederick funeral home. The rain had stopped, but wind scudded clouds across the sky.

The funeral was short. Called the evening before by the funeral director, the preacher hadn't known the Archers. His brief sermon lauded Frank's army service and assured the small audience Frank had done God's will in that awful war. Perhaps due to his short preparation time, perhaps due to her color, he didn't speak Carolyn's name,

122

referring to her as "the wife."

Carolyn was silent on the return trip home. John helped her up the steps, held the front door for her. As he took her coat she sighed, "Think I'll just go up and rest awhile."

The rest of the family sat in the front room and talked quietly.

John shook his head. "That wasn't much of a funeral. That preacher didn't know nothin' about Dad 'cept he was a soldier. And he didn't even know Mom's name."

Sherry said, "Well, it was real fast, he did the best he could, I think."

"Yeah, maybe. And I guess it's good there was some kinda service. A lotta the guys who died in the war didn't get that. I wish Joshua'd been able to come."

They sat in silence. The rain had returned, drizzle dripped off the edge of the roof, spattered in the dirt.

Sherry said, "Mom's sure torn up. He was everything to her. And she's aged so much, it's hard to believe. Her hair, last time we were here it was still black. Now it's very gray. And she walks bent. I hate to leave her alone here."

John said, "Y'know, there's no real reason you can't stay. I've gotta get back to the practice, but Regina can handle all the nurse duties for awhile."

Sherry thought a minute. "I guess so. It'd be good to be with her."

Della nodded. "I can stay too. I really haven't seen much of Grandma, we're so far away. And I'd like to. Is it okay if I stay?"

John replied. "I guess so. I'll miss you guys, but it'd be wonderful if Mom had people she loves here. She sure needs that now."

John returned to Rock Hill, and Sherry and Della stayed with Carolyn the rest of that summer. Della rambled the Maryland countryside, finding species that weren't down in Carolina. She filled a dozen jars of new bugs and lizards to add to the collection on her shelves.

Darlene was often with them, talking on the porch, sharing weekend suppers at the big house. The suppers and having the Carolina girls there helped to fill the huge vacancy that was Frank's memory, but regardless of the group's chatter, sadness lingered in Carolyn's eyes.

At the tenant house, Sherry and Darlene talked about Carolyn being alone in the big house.

Sherry said, "It's just gonna be so empty most of the time. I know you're close, and I'm sure you'll have her over when you can, but you know she's gonna be lonely."

"Yeah, I guess there's no way to avoid it. We'll do whatever we can, but she's gonna be lonely. He meant so much to her."

August 1919
John had driven to Buckeystown to pick Della and Sherry up. As they were putting the bags in the Ford's trunk, Darlene came to the car.

"I hate to see you leave, Sherry, but I guess it's time."

John asked, "How do you think she'll do without the girls here? I know you'll do what you can, but she'll miss them."

`"Well, I brought up an idea to her, that maybe it would be good if Allen and I came to live with her in the big house. Allen Junior could stay in the tenant house, take care of it. He's been gettin' pretty serious with a Frederick gal, I suspect the two of them'd be happy to have some privacy.

Sherry smiled. "Oh, that sounds like a wonderful idea. Keep on talking to her about it."

In October Darlene and Allen moved into the big house with Carolyn.

Rock Hill
Della was admitted to Winthrop College when she was seventeen. Like Rock Hill, it was growing rapidly, and soon became one of the

largest women's college in America. As in many American women's colleges, each year the campus celebrated the arrival of Spring by dancing around the Maypole, a tall pole which, dressed in white, the girls wrapped with colored ribbon as they skipped around it.

Students and faculty lounged on the grass, watching as the pole was gradually enveloped from top to bottom with ribbon. Half the dancers wrapped clockwise with white ribbon, half the reverse direction with red. Della was sitting next to Ernest Horton, her biology instructor. Ernest had moved to Rock Hill from Georgia at the beginning of the semester. Winthrop was his first teaching job out of college, so he was only four years older than Della. He wore a bowtie, his long black hair slicked over to one side.

Della giggled. "It's a penis."

"What?"

"Yes, this whole thing comes down from Greek legends, Dionysus and Aphrodite having a love affair. That ol' maypole is really a penis. Looks nice all stripey, doesn't it?"

"Now that you mention it, maybe, I hadn't really thought about it that way. Guess I should check my books of Greek legends. It's kind of skinny though."

"Well, I guess the school didn't want to be too literal. We're all chaste Southern gals, you know, Winthrop wouldn't want folks to see us dancing around a real dick."

Della loved school, particularly the sciences, and got excellent grades. Her relationship with Ernest became more personal as the semesters passed, and by the time she was a senior they'd begun a love affair. The school would've fired Ernest if the affair became known, so they avoided each other in Rock Hill and, except for classes, at the school.

Della's parents had no problem with the relationship, in fact were fond of Ernest. In warm weather, Della sometimes borrowed the family car and drove it to Lake Catawba. They trysted in the woods surrounding the lake, often camping for a weekend, spending the daylight hours swimming and walking through the woods, Della finding new insects in the leaf litter and identifying them in her field guide.

One Fall evening they lay in the tent. Pine needles scratched its roof as they fell in the wind.

"So dear, Georgia boy, tell me more about what growin' up there was like."

"Well, it was pretty easy. We lived on what was left of the plantation, I told you that. The war hurt us, Granddad had to sell off pretty much all the land, but we still had the house. Obviously, the slaves were gone, there was no more farmin' the place, but we had enough money to keep goin'. And Dad scratched up enough to send me off to college, make me a civilized man."

"Yes, you are civilized. And I love it."

They lay in silence. Ernest sighed.

"Yeah, dear old Georgia. I know you mostly know, but some of the stuff went on there, all through the South I guess, before the war, was pretty awful."

"You mean with the slaves?"

"Yeah, the slave women. Dad's father told him about the parties they had on the plantation. The guys'd get drunk and screw the slave gals for fun. Course that happened not just at parties."

"Fun, huh."

"Yeah, I'm sure the guys thought it was fun, sure the gals didn't. And Granddad evidently didn't have a bit of guilt about it, told Dad all about it. And the saddest thing, aside from not giving a damn about the women, Granddad told him it made economic sense."

"Economic?"

"Yup. One of the big values of a colored woman was as a baby maker. Didn't matter if the baby was black or brown or whatever, whether it was half black or one-hundredth black, it was a new slave, a new piece of property. Whether its daddy was a colored man or some partying white boy didn't matter. A new slave, worth good

126

money. Dad told me Granddad's father actually encouraged him and the boys, like 'git it on with her and make me some new ones! New ones with some good White blood in 'em! Help me with my investments!'"

Della shook her head. "God, that's sick."

She lay back. Pine needles skittered down the walls of the tent.

He's right, brown children as interest on an investment. That sure is sick. But God, I am so happy with him, and everything I see and hear and feel tells me he feels the same way. But I've never told him Grandma is colored. I really need to.

It wasn't camping weather a month later when they first stayed at a little inn on the outskirts of Charlotte. Snow blew as Ernest walked back to the car from the inn's office. As he pulled their bags from the back seat, Della asked, "So, any hassle registering, my fellow sinner?"

"No hassle, Mrs. Grandin."

"Mrs. Grandin, who's that?"

"For tonight that's you. We're Mr. and Mrs. Grandin."

"Mr. and Mrs. Grandin, eh. Guess that name's as good as any. For now."

He carried the bags to the door, unlocked it. "For now, huh?"

He threw the bags on one bed, sat on it, smiled. "I get the feeling you're thinkin' about what comes after now."

She tipped her head, nodded, "Could be. You been thinkin' any about that?"

"Well, yes I have."

She cocked her head, half-closed one eye. "Our next vacation?"

"Guess you could call it that. Only it'd be a whole lot longer than the vacations we've been takin' so far."

She clasped her hands together, looking intently at him. "Have you seen the pictures Mom and Dad have on the mantelpiece at home?"

"Yes."

"Did you see the one of the colored lady with the white man?"

"Yes."

"That's my grandmother and grandfather."

He nodded, smiled. "That's what your dad told me."

Della was silent. She looked at Ernest, still in his suit and bowtie on the bed. Her eyes brimmed with tears. She bent, reached for his tie, untied it, turned her back to him.

"Unbutton me."

He unbuttoned her dress, slid it down, stroked her shoulders, felt the smoothness of her skin. He slid the straps of her slip off. It fell to the floor. She turned to him, slid her underpants off and stood naked.

"You are so beautiful, my love. So very beautiful."

She pulled the covers down on the bed, lay back on it as he took his clothes off. He lay beside her, stroked her with his eyes and his hand. The tight curls on her pussy, her smooth slim belly, her breasts. Her nipples stood pointed, hard. He kissed one, then the other. Her hips reached up, she opened her legs. His hand stroked her, juice was slick on her pussy, on the insides of her legs.

He slid slowly into her, they both gasped.

"Open your eyes," he said. "Look at me."

She opened her eyes, "Ernest, Ernest, how I love you, I love you so."

"I know, and you know too." He kissed her forehead, her cheeks, her lips. "Open, open."

Her eyes fixed on his. "I am open, my love, so open to you."

Her body shuddered, her arms convulsed on his back, her legs pulling him deep inside her as she came on him. He watched her eyes

128

flutter closed as she cried out. "Oh love, oh love, oh love."

He tried to keep his eyes open as, with the most wonderful joy he'd ever known, he came into her.

****

They married in June of 1925. Ernest moved into the Archer house and continued teaching at Winthrop. Della attended Queens College in Charlotte, the closest college that offered significant courses in biology. With the science of herpetology in its infancy, college courses covered it skimpily. Della bought all the books she could find and studied at home.

Master's degree in hand, in 1927 she began teaching biology at Rock Hill Academy. As all Carolina schools at that time, it was segregated. All white. She arranged her schedule so her Academy classes fell on three days of the week. The other two she taught at all-black Emmet Scott School.

Tall, slender and dark-haired, Della's body was much like her mother's, and when it came to child-bearing, it behaved much the same way. During the first five years of her marriage, she had two miscarriages. Despite continuing to try for children, pregnancy escaped her.

Finally, on June 18 of 1943, Ernest Jr. came into the world. It was as if her female parts had simply needed more time than is typical—she was 39—to do their job. Her pregnancy was uneventful and Ernie, as he quickly became known, was perfect. Especially in his parents' eyes.

Della took two years off from teaching, loving motherhood with intensity proportional to the many years of waiting. In 1945 she hired a nanny to take care of Ernie and returned to teaching.

Ernie

When he was six, Ernie started first grade at Rock Hill Academy. Della was starting supper when he came into the kitchen.

"What're we havin' for supper, Mom?"

"Beef stew, honey. How was your day at school?"

"Okay, I guess.

"Mom, all the kids in my class are white. How come there's no colored kids?"

"Well honey, that's the way it is in our state. It's not fair, it's not right, but that's the way it is."

"Is it always gonna be like this?"

"I hope not, son. Things have been changing, but they don't change quickly."

Despite his mother teaching there, Ernie didn't have an easy time at the Academy. School parents were fully aware of his grandparents' multiracial medical practice and Della's work at Emmet Scott. And the possibility that Ernie wasn't totally White was sometimes discussed over the teachers' lunch. Inevitably, their attitudes flowed into the students.

Though Ernie's skin was white, it was heavily freckled. His lips were full and his hair was tightly curled. By fourth grade, he was abused frequently during recess.

"Where'd you get that nigger hair, white boy?"

"Why aintcha down at Scott with the rest of the darkies!"

On the second day of fifth grade, when Della got home from teaching, she found Ernie in the bathroom wiping blood from his nose.

"What happened?"

"Ted hit me."

"Who's Ted?"

"He's a big kid. He picks on me."

"Why?"

"Ah, just because he can I guess. And he makes fun of my hair."

Later that year, three boys grabbed him as he walked home from school. They held him down, took his sneakers off, tied the laces

130

together and threw them over a telephone line. He walked home in his socks. When Della came home from Scott he was on the front porch, his head in his hands.

"What's wrong, Ernie? Where are your shoes?"

"I hate this school! Why can't I go to Scott?"

"Honey, it's not as good a school as the Academy. You wouldn't get as good an education there."

"I still wish I could go there. At least I wouldn't hate it!"

In bed that evening, Della and Ernest talked about it, not for the first time.

Della frowned. "You know he's been having a rough time, and it seems to be getting worse. Some of these kids are just awful. It's one thing for grownups to deal with this bigoted state, but when you're just ten...?"

"Yeah, it is rough on him. I think it's the reason his grades aren't so good. Is there any possibility he could go to Scott?"

"Yeah, we could get him in there. He'd be the whitest kid in the school. And it wouldn't change anything after school, he'd still have to deal with the kids in the neighborhood."

"Yeah, the neighborhood. The Carolina neighborhood."

There was a long silence.

Della turned her face to him. "Would you be willing to move somewhere else?"

"Move? I don't want to move. I've got tenure at the college, and I enjoy teaching. And you, you've got good jobs teaching, and this's been your home your whole life. Where would we go?"

"How about the Buckeystown farm? It's near Frederick, not far from Baltimore and Washington, there's lots of jobs. And it's not Carolina!"

"Oh yeah, that farm's still in the family, isn't it, that's where those rent checks come from."

"Yeah, it's rented out, but it's still ours. A big old farmhouse

131

with a tenant house. And it's pretty country, the Potomac River, the Monocacy River, and plenty of mountains."

"I dunno. It's a heck of a change. Do you think it's worth it?"

"I think it's worth a try, at least a looksee."

During supper that weekend they talked about it with John and Sherry.

John said, "We'd sure miss you, but it's not like you'd be in Alaska or something. What do you know about jobs up there?"

"I'm sure I could teach, and Ernest probably could too. Buckeystown's pretty close to Washington, there's lots of government jobs. I think it's worth a try."

During Spring break, Ernest and Della drove to Frederick and stayed in a motel. They scrutinized the Washington and Baltimore papers for job possibilities, cutting clippings for teaching possibilities in the Frederick County schools and Hood College. Ernest found an ad for a biology teacher at Frederick High School.

"So Della, this sounds good, Frederick High's looking for a biology teacher, their current one is retiring at the end of the year. The pay's as good as what I'm getting at Winthrop, and I've certainly got the credentials. Think I should interview?"

"Of course. Maybe after awhile you'll end up teaching Ernie."

"There's also an opening at Lincoln School, it's the.Black school, covers all twelve grades."

"All twelve grades! Ah yes, how could I forget, this may not be Carolina, but it's not New York, the schools are still segregated. God, when will it end?"

"I think if we do move here, we should just send Ernie to the White schools. If it's anything like Carolina, they're a lot better than the Black ones, and I don't think he'll catch any of the shit he's getting at the Academy."

"I'm pretty sure you're right. He shouldn't have trouble passing."

Della was paging through the Frederick News. "Ernest, look at this ad. Jungleland Snake Farm is looking for someone to manage its reptile exhibits!"

"Never heard of it. Where is it?"

"About ten miles north of here. Listen to this. 'Jungleland Snake Farm houses one of the finest collections of snakes in the country, including Indian hooded cobras, a 14-foot king cobra, Gaboon vipers, ball pythons, regal pythons, a yellow anaconda, a reticulated python, diamondback rattlers, cottonmouth water moccasins, coral snakes and copperheads."

"Just up your alley."

"That's not all, dear. They also have, and I quote, 'beaded lizards, Gila monsters, sooty mangley monkeys from Africa, rhesus monkeys from India, spider monkeys from South America, a chimpanzee, and a 125-pound Galapagos tortoise.'"

"I didn't know you were into sooty mangley monkeys."

"Well, they're not my specialty, for sure, wiseass. And look, they have public demonstrations of rattlesnake milking and alligator wrestling each weekend!"

"You ready to wrestle an alligator?"

"No, but I don't think the reptile manager has to wrestle. Probably some strong young guy."

Photo courtesy Catoctin Wildlife Reserve and Zoo

Two days later Della shook hands with Gordon Gaver, who'd started Jungleland in 1933, confirming her agreement to start as the zoo's reptile manager at the end of school year. Frederick High was thrilled with Ernest's teaching credentials, and made it clear the biology teacher position would be his when the next school year started.

They visited the McAllisters in Buckeystown and talked about moving into the big house. Both Allen McAllister Senior and his wife Darlene had died, so that house stood empty. Allen Jr., now with his wife Josephine and son Tom, was still in the tenant house and farming the fields. He'd been keeping an eye on the big house and would be glad to have them come live in it.

Back in Rock Hill, Della and John submitted their resignations and in June, with new jobs waiting, the Hortons moved to Buckeystown.

1952
Buckey**stown**

Eleven-year-old Tom McAllister is happy when his dad Allen tells him the Hortons will be moving into the big house next door and they have a boy his age. Tom loves the countryside but there isn't much company. The Buckeystown area is mainly farms, with houses and barns scattered over the land, and no boys his age nearby.

The day after the Hortons moved in, Tom got his chores done early, got his fishing rod and knocked on the farmhouse door. Della answered.

"Well good morning, Tom, it's good to see you."

"Good mornin', Miz Horton, is Ernie here?"

"Yes. Ernie!" Ernie came up behind her.

"Ernie, this is Tom from next door."

Tom smiled. "Hi, you wanna go fishin'?"

"Yeah. Mom, where's my fishin' pole?"

"A bunch of that stuff is out in the shed, still in boxes."

Five minutes later, Della called after the boys as, poles in hand, they headed across the yard toward Fingerboard Road.

"Have a good time, boys."

Tom asked, "Have you seen the river?"

"No. I mean, I know it's there but I've never been to it."

They stopped at the edge of a farm field and dug worms where the field bordered the trees lining the Monocacy River, then clambered and slid down its bank. The river was still chilly from Spring and the Catoctin Mountain streams that fed it. But not too chilly for wading. They shed their socks and sneakers and waded in knee-deep, casting bobbers.

Bites came quickly, and in an hour a string of bluegills and bass trailed from a stringer.

"So, whaddya think of Maryland? Like it?

"I guess. This river sure is fulla fish."

So began the most important friendship the boys had through their school years. Tom often stayed over at Ernie's, sleeping on a spare mattress on his floor. On sweaty summer nights they'd drag a mattress out the window onto the porch roof, watch the moon and listen to the owls holler and the peepers peep till they fell asleep.

Summer was river time. The Monocacy wasn't great in winter, you couldn't count on the ice being thick enough to walk or skate, but the other seasons were fine. Except when storms raged through, it was gentle, great for swimming. It wasn't very wide, a hundred feet or so at most places, nor very deep, you could wade most of it. Remnants of Catoctin Mountain, boulders fractured and scattered over millions of years, some broad and flat-topped, lay in the lazily swirling water.

A late July afternoon, the boys stretched on towels spread on a boulder in the middle of the river, sun on their browning bodies. It was sweaty hot in the fields and the towns, but the river cured that. Tom pushed himself into the water, dunked his head and stood up, water dripping from his hair onto his shoulders.

"Didja have anything this neat down in Carolina?"

"We did have a river, but it was different, not so many rocks. There was a lot more sand, easier to walk on the bottom."

"How come you moved here?"

"Well, part of it was I got hassled some in school, takin' some shit."

"How come?"

There was a long silence. Ernie's mind turned and turned. He could just say his mom got a job up here. But should he tell Tom his big reason?

"I guess you know the folks down there have a thing about colored people, right?"

"Yeah."

"If I tell you somethin' will you promise to keep it a secret?"

136

"Sure."

"You swear?"

"I swear, yeah."

"Well, my great-grandma was colored."

"Wow. Well, you sure don't look colored to me."

"They look harder down south. They figgered it out 'cause of my hair, I guess."

"Your hair?"

"Yeah, 'cause it's all kinky, like a colored person."

"They did bad shit to you cause of your hair? That's pretty stupid."

Ernie slid off the rock and lay on his back in the water.

"They're pretty stupid down there. Lots of shitty people."

Tom joined him in the water. They floated in the Monocacy as the sun slid across the summer sky to set west of Sugarloaf Mountain.

****

When high school time came, the boys rode the bus together. They were both on the track team, and Ernie came to watch Tom when the wrestling team had matches. After school they lifted weights in Ernie's basement, building biceps and talking about girls.

They both wore the costume typical of teen boys in that era, jeans and a plain white teeshirt. Ernie's shirt usually had a pack of Camels rolled up in one sleeve, a squarish lump on his left shoulder.

He loved music, particularly the rock songs that updated old blues songs. He pestered his parents and for his fourteenth birthday, they got him an old Favilla guitar. He spent hours in his room, learning chords and building calluses on his fingers, lifting the needle onto and off old 45s, scribbling lyrics and figuring out the chords B.B King used.

By eleventh grade, cars became a major focus of both their lives. A car gave status, a place to make out, maybe even get laid. Tom's uncle gave him a '49 Chrysler when he turned 16, old enough to drive. It ran well, but was certainly not the kind of sexy wheels the guys ran up and down Market Street, glasspack mufflers snarling, radios blaring, or showed off in the drive-in burger joint on Route 40.

Tom had done what he could with it. A seagull feather dangled on a chain from the rearview mirror. The handle from a Lowenbrau keg, a whiff of international cool, replaced the plain gearshift knob.

Mal

1958

Frederick

In their junior year, Mal Alexopoulos came through the Frederick High homeroom door. He looked like nobody else in the room. His hair was a "DA," a "duck's ass," long and slicked back on the sides. Big for his age, six feet and close to 200 pounds. The school didn't allow the clothes he liked to wear, but when he wasn't there his garb was motorcycle—black engineer boots with brass buckles, jeans with a chain hanging from a front belt loop to a side pocket, and a leather jacket with chrome snaps and clips.

He was at Frederick High because he'd been kicked out of Saint John's, the local Catholic school. Despite his appearance, he wasn't a tough guy, but a fight at Saint John had gotten him expelled. In the school's 300-plus student body there were only a handful of colored kids, and they took some abuse. One day after gym, Bill Lundy, a small colored kid, was in the locker room getting ready to shower. Art Murphy and two other white kids grabbed him, held him down on the floor and pulled his underpants over his arms, jamming his balls up against his crotch. He yelled, Mal heard the commotion.

A minute later, one white kid had a broken nose. Blood poured from another's mouth onto his teeshirt. The other two got the hell out of there, went to the gym teacher. Mal was expelled the next day.

Tom met Mal when he joined the wrestling team. He was in the unlimited weight class, and despite being smaller than some of the guys he wrestled, he lost only one match during his first season. They were together at wrestling practice and matches all through the winter, but hadn't spent any time together out of school.

In late March Tom and Ernie ran into Mal at a beer store. Tom was buying beer with a fake ID, a Texas driver's license that claimed he was 20. The guy who ran the store didn't give a damn who he sold beer to. He just wanted to sell it.

The boys put their beer in Tom's Chrysler and drove to the Dry Rez. Bordered on one side by railroad tracks, it was a several-acre depression filled with scrub trees and bushes, with ten-foot berms around it. It had once been a reservoir, but now it was dry, a great place for boys to drink beer. And it was a lot cheaper to take a case of Old German beer (two bucks) to the Dry Rez than to pay a dime for a dinky glass at a bar.

It was a warm windless night. They sat in a clump of scrub trees and sipped beers.

"So Mal, how'd you get kicked out of St. John?" Ernie asked.

"Ah, Art Murphy and some other assholes were pickin' on a little colored kid. Just cause he was colored, and because they could."

"So?"

"So they weren't all that big themselves, and, uh, I pointed that out to them. Not with words."

"That got you thrown out?"

"Yup. Murphy told some bullshit story to the gym teacher, and I guess he convinced Father Bellotti I should get tossed."

They sipped their beers and crumpled cans into the underbrush. A train rattled by.

"You had a hell of a wrestling season, man," Tom said to Mal.

"Yeah, I like wrestling. Just one on one, don't have to rely on someone else doing his job. You do yours, and maybe you'll win. Not always, but ..."

"Well you sure did."

"Well, how 'bout your season, champ?" Tom had won the

league championship in his weight class.

"Yeah, it was good. And luck was with me when I needed it. Can I use your churchkey again?"

Along with his keys, Mal's can opener hung from the chrome chain clipped to his jeans. He scooted his butt closer to Tom and stretched the chain out. Tom sank the opener's triangular point into a can. It hissed and foamed over the can's sides.

"Y'know, you oughta come and lift with us at my house," Ernie said to Mal.

"I didn't know you guys were lifting."

"Yeah, some days after school, some on weekends."

"Well, that'd be good. Can always use some more muscles." Mal sank his churchkey into another beer. "I appreciate it. And I appreciate you guys. I don't know many of the guys at school yet."

"Well, lots of 'em aren't worth knowing," Ernie replied. "There's some pretty snotty kids there."

"Yeah."

August 1958

It's a hot humid Saturday, haze veiling Catoctin Mountain to the west as the boys once again escape summer's heat at the Monocacy. But this summer they're a trio. A swing now adorns the river's edge. Tom had shinnied up a sycamore and tied a rope to a branch that leaned out over the water. You carry the rope up the bank, then swing down with your feet braced on the knot at the rope's end. When you're way out over the river, you let go and splash. Mal is the champion swinger, hitting the water a good ten feet past the best the

140

others can do.

All three had part-time jobs, so the river wasn't an everyday thing, but it was often, weekends and long summer evenings. As an evening approached they lay on their towels on a flat midriver rock.

Tom said, "Y'know, it doesn't get much better than this."

"Well, maybe. I can think of one way it could be," Ernie answered.

Mal, spread in the summer sun, asked, "And that is?"

"Geraldine Edwards lyin' here with me. Without any clothes. And nothin' against you guys, but with you not here."

Mal shook his head. "Ah, you don't wanna be on this rock naked, anybody comes by they'll hoot at you. Maybe take pictures."

"Alright then, maybe not on this rock, it's too damn hard. Maybe over there, a nice soft place on a blanket in the shade."

"And then?"

"Hell, you know what then. Getting laid!"

Tom smiled. "Well, you lemme know when you've got Geraldine convinced to come to the river with you and I'll stay home. Or maybe I'll hide in the bushes with my camera."

A week later, the next Saturday morning, the boys stand at the foot of Sugarloaf Mountain. At twelve hundred feet, it's a baby compared to the four-thousand-foot Appalachians in Maryland's far west.

Nonetheless, the westerly face of the baby looms above them, a sheer rock cliff bordered by clusters of oak, hemlock and pine. The pines at the top of the cliff are stunted and twisted, their trunks bent westward by the prevailing

141

wind, westerly branches reaching toward the valley, eastern branches small, nearly devoid of needles. A jumble of boulders borders the bottom of the rock face on the left.

Tom points to a broad opening, little more than a foot high, grinning at them from the base of the white stone face.

The entrance to Sugarloaf Cave.

The day before, Tom had called Mal, keeping mystery in what he said.

"Mal, you're gonna like this, it's a real adventure, but you gotta be prepared. We gotta start early, it may take all day. Bring flashlights, a couple if you got 'em, and your kneepads from wrestling."

"Flashlights and kneepads. That's pretty weird, what're we gonna be doing?"

"Trust me, you'll like it. And bring a jacket, an old one that doesn't matter if it gets dirty. And wear boots."

He talked to Ernie after his phonecall with Mal and said essentially the same thing. Mystery.

At 7 Saturday morning, they met at Fingerboard Road and walked down to the river. Tom sat against an oak and pulled a small brass-colored thing with a silver reflector from his backpack.

"What the hell is that?"

"It's a miner's lamp."

"We're goin' mining?"

"Not quite." He screwed the top off the lamp, showed them how water trickled from the upper chamber into the lower, which was filled with calcium carbide chunks. He screwed the lamp together, adjusted a knob on top and lit a match. A small tongue of flame flickered from a jet in the middle of the reflector.

"Before they had stuff like batteries and flashlights, this is how you got to see in the dark. It's acetylene gas. Dad tells me they used to have bigger lamps like this on the streets in Frederick. They even used 'em on cars before they got batteries and lights."

"Well, that's pretty cool, but if we're not goin' mining, where are we goin'?" Mal asked.

"Sugarloaf." Tom pointed across the river to the mountain. "The Sugarloaf cave."

It had taken an hour to walk the three miles to the mountain, shedding their boots to cross shallow Bennett Creek. At the mountain's base, Tom lit the carbide lamp and hung it on a strap around his head. "It looks tight, you gotta crawl to get in but it opens up good once you're in. Now you know why the kneepads. And put your jackets on."

Tom asked, "How'd you find out about this place?"

"One of the guys at school told me about it. C'mon, let's do it."

He lay on his belly and scooted through the narrow slot. Ernie followed, but Mal was big enough that his chest jammed in the slot.

"Hey guys, I'm stuck! Man, this doesn't feel good. How many tons of rock I got pressin' on my ribcage? This ain't good! What if this damn mountain decides it's gonna slump down while I'm under it."

Ernie crawled to Mal. "These mountains don't slump very often. Gimme your hands and I'll give you a pull."

Ernie's pull did the job, Mal wriggled through.

"Thanks, man. I hope I can get back outta here."

Past the entrance, the cave opened into a large room. Light from the flashlights and lamp shone off the cave's walls and ceiling. It was cool, almost cold despite the near-ninety temperature outside.

Ernie wrinkled his nose. "What's that smell?"

"You'll see in the next room."

A hole at the base of the wall to their right led to a short passageway leading to a second, even larger room. The smell, of

143

vague rot, acidic dryness, was stronger. Tom tipped his head back, pointing his lamp at the ceiling.

Hundreds of bats hung from it. Some twitched and shifted. Mal's eyes widened. "Wow."

"Pretty neat, huh." Tom whispered. "They hang out here in daytime, fly out and eat bugs at night. Talk quietly, we don't want to get 'em waked up and flyin' around. We might get guanoed."

"Guanoed?"

"Batshitted. You see all that brown stuff on the floor, that's batshit. Guano. They use it for fertilizer some places. C'mon, there's somethin' else I want you to see."

Tom crawled back into the first room, then to a second passageway. Narrow and long, it pitched downward, its walls getting wetter and wetter as the boys crawled.

"Hey, how far we goin' down this anyhow?" Ernie asked.

"Just a little further, hang in there."

The passage opened into a third room, smaller than the prior ones, with darker walls. And much wetter. Water-slicked cones hung from the ceiling. Below each hanging cone, another, reversed in shape, reached up from the cave floor.

Tom said, "Know what these are?"

Ernie nodded, "Stalactites and stalagmites. Very cool."

"And they're old. I mean old. After I was here the first time I got a book from the library about them. It takes about 200 years for one of them to grow an inch. Look at these guys, some of 'em are four feet long, so that's like what?"

Mal frowned, spinning numbers in his head. "Jeez. Ninety-six thousand years. So this cave's been here like this for maybe a hundred thousand years."

A drop of water hung on the tip of a stalactite, a patient stalagmite below it. They watched. It hung.

The boys crawled back into the first room. Shattered stone fragments covered its floor. Sunlight gleamed through the cave entrance. As Mal kneeled to crawl through it, something stabbed his knee.

"Ouch! What the hell is this?"

A triangular piece of stone had cut through his pant leg and stuck him. He pulled it from his pants.

"Jeez, it looks like an arrowhead."

Ernie held his hand out. "Wow, lemme see it."

He turned it in his hand. "I've never found one, but my grandpa told me about 'em. It's flint."

Tom reached out. "Let's see it. Boy, it's sharp as hell."

"Yeah, doesn't rust like metal, this thing's just as sharp as when an Indian chipped a piece of flint to make it."

"Is it old?"

"Hard to tell. It could be thousands of years old, but it might be from when the Tuscarora were here after American troops kicked them off their land in Carolina."

"Didn't they have metal by then?"

"I guess they did. Maybe this was just from some old guy who liked the old ways."

They walked and crawled back to the cave mouth. Tom went out first, ready to give Mal a pull if he needed it, but this time he wriggled through without assistance. The sun was blinding after the cave's gloom, and the day's heat hit them like fire. They were dripping sweat as they walked down the mountain.

"Man, that river's gonna feel good," said Ernie.

It was a downhill walk, and the river beckoned every step, so they got to the Monocacy quickly. They stripped to their underwear and jumped in.

"Ah man, does this feel good!" Tom said.

In just a few minutes, they'd cooled down, and lay on their favorite river rock in the sun.

Ernie sat up, turned to Mal. "Mal, lemme see that arrowhead again." He turned it in his hand. "You guys know about blood brothers?"

"Not really."

"Well, it's somethin' you do as a sign that you really are brothers. You cut yourself and let your blood mix."

"I never heard of it," said Mal.

"Well, it's been around for centuries. My dad teaches some of that stuff, he told me about it. Says it was a thing in a whole lot of cultures in Europe, and China, and a lotta other places. It says you're brothers and always will be, even though you're not from the same mother. I mean, you can't choose your family brothers, but you do choose your blood brothers."

Tom's eyebrows raised. "That sounds pretty cool."

"You wanna do it?"

"Yeah," said Mal, "I think that'd be great. With that arrowhead?"

"Well, doncha think that'd be neat, becoming blood brothers with an Indian arrowhead that may be hundreds, even thousands of years old?"

He stood up on the rock, holding the base of the blade in his left hand, hesitated a moment, then slid its tip across the bottom of the deltoid muscle on his right arm. The horizontal cut bled. He handed the arrowhead to Mal. Mal cut himself at the same place, gave the arrowhead to Tom. Blood flowed down onto their triceps. They turned so their arms met in the center of their circle.

Their blood mixed.

1959

The boys' time in high school nears its end. Despite both his parents being educators, Ernie's been a poor student, erratic getting homework done, attention wandering in class. Except for shop. He enjoys working wood and

146

metal with the shop's power tools. Shop class introduces him to fiberglass, and he and Tom use it to customize Tom's old Chrysler. Using fiberglass and body putty, they "bullnose" the hood, "french" the headlights, then repaint the car. Ernie decorates the trunk and hood with gold pinstriping atop the Royal Blue paint.

When they graduate, Tom's near the top of the class, Mal's in the middle, Ernie's close to the bottom.

Tom was admitted to Frederick Community College, but Ernie was turned down due to his poor grades. His parents urged him to apply to Winthrop College. Although the school was technically a women's college, a few boys attended classes there. His family's connections still carried weight at the school, and he was admitted. Founded in 1886, Winthrop had changed some since its name was Winthrop Normal and Industrial College of South Carolina, but its racial policies hadn't. In 1959, all its students were white.

Or at least not obviously colored.

Ernie dreaded returning to Rock Hill. He shared his feelings with the boys.

"It's just a shitty place, y'know, like backward. And mean. Imagine *Leave It To Beaver,* only Beaver carries a switchblade and hates Negroes. The girls are all snobby and the guys have their groups. If you haven't been part of a group since junior high, you're never gonna be."

Mal had taken a job with a local construction company. "I can see if there's a place in one of the crews where I work if you want."

147

"Nah, my parents want me to go to college. My mom went to Winthrop, and my grandfather used to be a big mucketymuck there. So I guess I gotta go."

"What are you gonna major in?" Tom asked.

"I dunno. Whatever."

Rock Hill

It would be a gross understatement to say Ernie didn't distinguish himself at Winthrop. In fact, he seldom attended class. He'd taken a part-time job at Morgan's car repair shop, where he befriended Johnny Burnette, a young colored mechanic. Johnny raced his '58 Chevy at the local drag strip, and Ernie learned a lot watching Johnny set the car up.

He'd carried his guitar down to Winthrop. Given the time he spent playing with it and the cars, it wasn't a surprise that his grades—two Incompletes—landed him on academic probation at the end of the first semester.

An old man Johnny knew had a rusty '32 Ford coupe out behind his house. Looked pretty awful, the engine didn't work, but most of the body was still solid. The old man didn't know the car, called a Deuce by car lovers, was valuable. Ernie convinced the fella to sell it to him for $50, and the boys towed it to Morgan's.

After many hours of work, all the the Deuce's body rust was gone. Hand-rubbed crimson lacquer replaced the faded black paint. Channeled low to the ground, the car was raked forward as if ready to jump. The old engine, a flathead V-8, was beyond repair, so they hauled it to the junkyard.

One day while they were working on the Deuce, Johnny mentioned that his dad worked at the Rock Hill quarry. Ernie's ears perked up.

"So, they use dynamite at the quarry?"

"Hell yes. Lots of it, there's blasts going off just about every day."

"Sure would be fun if we could get some. Lot more fun than firecrackers!"

A week later Johnny came to Morgan's with four sticks of dynamite in his toolbox.

"Wow Johnny, how'd you get it?"

"Let's just say they don't always keep the explosive locker locked, leave it at that. Pretty neat, huh?"

"So whaddya wanna do with it? Let's make a little bit of noise over at the college, wake some of those snotty kids up."

A little after one the next morning they drove to the edge of the Winthrop campus, parked Johnny's Chevy facing for a quick getaway, and walked down Sumter Avenue to a clump of trees off Oakland Avenue. Wired tightly together, the dynamite sticks were hidden under Johnny's shirt. It was a cool May night, windless, nobody on the street. A few lights shone from North Dormitory windows, kids studying late for finals.

They kneeled next to a big oak tree. Ernie uncoiled the fuse from under his jacket, whispered, "You figure this is enough?"

"I guess."

Using his teeth, Johnny crimped a detonator tube on one end of the fuse, inserted the fuse and tube deep in one of the sticks, and lay the bundle on the ground by the oak.

"Okay, you wanna light it?"

Ernie flicked his cigarette lighter and held it to the fuse. It fizzed and stopped. Johnny cut an inch off the fuse with his penknife. Ernie lit it again.

It spat sparks and kept spitting. The boys ran across Oakland, down Sumter, got to the car just before the blast.

It sounded like two blasts, the first coming straight to them, the second an echo off the three-story brick wall of North Dormitory. Both were very loud. Leaves on the tree over the Chevy fluttered as

149

the shock wave passed by.

Giggling, they got in the car, shut the doors as quietly as possible, and eased away down Sumter Avenue.

The next morning the campus police and the York County Sheriff's office inspected North Dormitory. A quarter of its East-facing windows had been blown out. Nobody was hurt since almost all the students had been in bed, but glass was scattered on dorm room furniture, beds and floors. Bark was stripped off the oak tree above the blast site, a shallow hole three feet across. Students gathered around it. And some locals, including Arthur Burnette, Johnny's dad.

When Johnny got home from work, Arthur cornered him.

"What kind of damn fool are you, boy? I shoulda known you didn't come visit me at work just to say hello. You stole that dynamite, didn't you, and set it off . What the hell did you do that for?"

Johnny said nothing.

"And why'd you go do that at Winthrop. If you wanted to make a big bang, you coulda set it off in a field or something. It was that white boy Ernie's idea, wasn't it? He goes to school there."

Johnny said nothing, but his face said a lot.

Only two companies in York County were authorized to use dynamite, and Tank Rogers quickly pinpointed the quarry as the source. Arthur, one of only two colored employees, was the first he questioned.

"Arthur, ain't it pretty strange that four sticks of dynamite go missing from your quarry and a blast goes off at Winthrop a week later? How do you think that coulda happened?"

"I guess I shoulda come to you about it, sir. I just found out, last night at supper, that Johnny took that dynamite. I don't know why he did it, just bein' a dumb kid I guess. But any damage was done, I'll pay to have it fixed."

"If you wanna keep your job here, you have that boy down to my office tomorrow morning."

It didn't take long for Sheriff Rogers to get the whole story out of Johnny. Ernie was expelled from Winthrop the next day.

Tom's phone rang three days later. It was Ernie.

"Hey Tom, I could use some help."

"What kind of help?"

"Well, seems like I'm not welcome here at Winthrop any more, need to come back home. Think you could come and pick me up?"

"What happened?"

Ernie told him about the dynamite, the windows of the girls' dorm, the whole story.

"So, can you come down, pick me up?"

"Man, that's a long way. Can't you just take a bus or something?"

"Well, not if I'm gonna bring the Deuce back."

"A Deuce? I didn't know you had a Deuce."

"Yup. Bought her for almost nothing, been workin' on her since last October. She's lookin' pretty fine. All she needs is a motor."

"No motor, huh? No wonder you called me."

"Well, yeah. I need your help. How about you get a tow bar, put it on your car, come on down here and we'll tow her back there?"

"Rock Hill's a helluva run, man, gotta be over 400 miles each way."

"Hey, I'll pay the gas. Whaddya say? Your semester's over, right? What else you got to do?"

Tom was quiet a moment.

"Okay. What's a blood brother for? "

"Why don't you see if our other blood brother would like to come along?"

Tom called Mal and, indeed, he could get time off work for a Southern adventure. They left early in the morning a day later, a tow bar fitted to the Chrysler's back bumper, a gallon of oil and two jugs of water in the trunk. Despite its age and miles, the Chrysler purred along the highway, smoking a bit, headed south. Every couple of hours they stopped to top up the radiator and add oil.

They pulled up in front of Morgan's garage as the sun was setting. Ernie had taken up sleeping on an air mattress in one of its back rooms.

"Let's see this Deuce of yours," said Mal.

Behind the garage, Ernie pulled off the tarp that covered the car.

"Wow, that's some paint job."

"Yeah, took awhile. Sprayed eight coats of lacquer, then hand-rubbed to get that shine."

"It's fucking gorgeous."

"Yeah. All it needs is a motor. I'll deal with that after we get it back home."

He brought two sixpacks out of the office fridge.. They sat on tires, sipped, and planned the trip home.

The next day, the Deuce attached solidly to the Chrysler's back bumper, engine topped with oil and radiator filled, the boys started north. The day was hot and clear, heat waves shimmered from the pavement. Rock Hill's streets gave way quickly to country roads. After they crossed the Catawba River, farm fields bordered the road.

"Is all that white stuff stuck in the weeds cotton?" said Tom.

"Yup," said Ernie. "When they pick it and transport it, some blows out of the truck."

"Geez, it's everywhere!"

"Yeah, this part of the country it is everywhere. There was more when I was a kid, but there's still a hell of a lot planted. They use mechanical harvesters now, but it used to be picked totally by hand. You'd see gangs of colored folks in the field picking the cotton out of the bolls, dragging big burlap bags behind them. A full bag

152

weighed a hundred pounds. It was tough, tough work. The spikes on the cotton plants ripped up their hands."

"You remember seeing that?" asked Mal.

"Yeah. In fact my grandfather had cotton land down here, had gangs workin' for him."

"What happened to it?"

"He sold it to a guy, a civil war vet with one arm. My mom said they got to be real good friends, even though they fought on different sides in the war."

A flapping noise interrupted them. A corner of the tarp over the Deuce had come unfastened and was whacking its fender. Tom pulled to the side of the road.

Mal helped Ernie tighten the cords holding the tarp. "Growing up down here sure sounds different than in Maryland."

"Yeah, sure was, specially when it came to how the colored were treated. It just didn't make sense. I mean, back when there was slavery, even after it, they'd classify a person by how much negro blood they had. They had categories with names like mulatto, quadroon, octoroon, all sorts of names. If you were a quadroon, a quarter of you was negro."

"They kept track of all that shit?"

"Yeah. But when it came to being a slave, it didn't matter how much of you was colored. Like, one drop of negro blood would make me not a whole person, I'd be like a mule, someone could own me. And even weirder, a lot of slaves bought their way out of it. If somehow they scraped enough money together to pay off their owner, they wouldn't be a mule anymore, they'd be a free person. Is that weird or what?"

"Guess that's the power of money."

"Yeah. You'd think only god could turn a mule into a man, but turns out money can too. At least it could in those days."

"Dunno that it's any different today."

North Carolina's cotton-dusted country roads gradually gave way to the suburbs, then to Charlotte. Idling along Charlotte's city roads, the Chrysler's radiator spouted steam. The boys stopped in front of the bus station, filled their jug from its water fountain.

Radiator topped up, they picked up Route 29 heading north toward Greensboro. To the west, the sun sank through shimmering heat waves veiling the Smoky Mountains.

They didn't make it far. Twenty miles north of Charlotte, a cloud of steam enveloped the front of the car. Tom pulled over just past a sign announcing they were coming into China Grove. Tom popped the hood. A steam stream blasted from the radiator.

Mal shook his head. "This ain't good. Water's comin' out as fast as we can put it in."

"Yeah. If we weren't towing it might be OK, but it's just too much for this old radiator," Tom replied. "We're gonna have to get the sucker plugged somehow."

"Just our luck. Late as it is, everything's gonna be closed up. That's assuming there is anything in this dinky town."

A bright red Chevy pickup came up 29 toward them, rolled past the Chrysler and pulled over. It growled through shiny chrome exhaust stacks as the engine revved twice, muttered to a stop. A confederate flag decal covered part of the cab's back window.

The driver was in his 20s, blond hair brushing the collar of his Levi jacket. A cigarette dangled from the corner of his mouth.

"Looks like y'all got some trouble. And you're a long way from home." He'd seen the Maryland plates on the Chrysler.

Ernie's Carolina accent came back in a hurry. "Yeah, radiator's got a hole. It's tired 'a towin'."

"Whatcha towin'?"

"A Deuce. Bringing it up from Rock Hill."

"A Deuce? Let's see it."

Ernie untied the cords holding the tarp and pulled it back.

"Wow! Guess you got some time in that paint job. "

"Yeah. You know any place where we might get the radiator patched?"

"I can do it. But not tonight, my shop's closed up."

"Tomorrow?"

"Yeah, I can probably solder it up tomorrow. Tell you what, if you want you can bring the car to my place, it's less than a mile down the road, you can make it that far."

"Well, thanks. Sure would be better than hangin' out along the road here." Ernie held out his hand. "I'm Ernie Horton."

"I'm Tad. Tad Custis."

The radiator had stopped steaming. Tom retrieved the water jug, filled it back up. Tad got in his truck, peeled out, and the boys followed.

Tad lived in a double-wide with a saggy wooden porch place surrounded by a scatter of buildings and vehicles. His shop, an old garage next to it, cars in various states of repair, axles, ratty car bench seats and a gleaming Harley-Davidson. As Tom stepped out of the Chrysler he was greeted by a hound with long floppy ears and mournful eyes. He scratched the dog's head.

Tad said, "Buster's about as useful as tits on a bull. He was supposed to be a rabbit dog, but he wouldn't know a rabbit from a rock. You guys hungry? There's a good pizza shop in town."

Pizza was a fine idea. They pooled money, Mal and Tad headed to town. Ernie and Tom checked out the Harley and the cars. One was a '50 Ford Tudor with crimson flames decorating the hood.

Ernie slid his hand over the front of the hood. The original ornament was gone, replaced by a smooth curve. "Man, this is a great bullnose job. Tad really knows what he's doing with fiberglass. You can't tell where the metal ends and the glass begins." They moved to a '40 Plymouth 2-door coupe, not in great shape. The door panels were badly rusted. Springs poked through the front seat upholstery.

"Got his work cut out for him here."

In half an hour the pizzas and two six-packs arrived. The boys

155

lounged on the bench seats, eating, sipping beer. Rock music blared from the truck radio.

Tad nodded at the Deuce. "How'd you come by this gem? And how come you're taking it up north?"

Ernie related the whole story. His Carolina family, dynamite on the Winthrop campus, moving to Buckeystown. Tad listened intently. "You've bounced around some, huh. What's it like living up north?"

"Not all that much different than here, 'cept it's gettin' pretty built up. A lot of the people work in Washington. So, you think you can get the radiator fixed tomorrow?"

"Probly. I gotta see how bad the leak is. If it's not too bad I can solder it. If it's bad you may need a new radiator."

"Think you can get us back on the road sometime tomorrow?"

"Like I said, we'll see. And you may not want to rush back on the road anyhow. I'm having a party tomorrow night, with a good band outta Charlotte. You might just want to hang around, maybe you could pick a few songs with them. You can crash here if you want. Not that you've got a whole lot of choice. But you're welcome."

The Big Bopper crooned from WGIV.

Chantilly lace and a pretty face and a pony tail hangin' down,
A wiggle and a walk and a giggle and a talk
make the world go round
There ain't nothing in the world
Like a big-eyed girl make me act so funny
make me spend my money
Make me feel real loose like a long-neck goose
Like a girl oh baby that's what I like

The pizza and beer was gone, clearly time to sack out. Tad headed into the trailer.

"So whaddya think of this guy?" Ernie asked.

Tom said, "Seems pretty up-front, pretty generous. I mean,

letting a bunch of out-of-state strangers camp on his lawn. Seems like a nice guy to me."

"How about that Confederate flag on his truck?" Mal said.

"You see a lotta them down here. You wanna stay for the party tomorrow?"

Tom said, "Sounds like a good idea to me. I mean, what's the rush?"

Tom laid down on the Chrysler's front seat. Mal stretched his lanky frame over the back seat leaving one door open. His feet hung out. Ernie inflated his air mattress in Tad's shop and picked on his guitar until sleepiness laid it down.

Caroline

The Carolina sun woke the boys early. Tad brought coffee out. Tom poured a cup, nodded at Tad. "Thanks man, thanks for lettin' us stay and everything. Maybe we oughta pick up some food, and maybe something for the party."

Tad said, "Well that'd be great. If you wanna use my truck, go ahead."

Mal and Tom headed into town. Ernie watched as Tad began work on the Chrysler radiator. It quickly became obvious it was a lost cause, a new one would be needed. Phoning, Tad found one at a Chrysler dealer in Charlotte and arranged for pickup the next day.

That afternoon the band—keyboard, guitar, bass and a girl drummer—set up in front of Tad's shop. The keyboard player and the drummer were colored. The partygoers drifted in, some with folding chairs. Others dragged car seats, an old sofa, two overstuffed chairs onto the lawn. Tad laid an old mattress over truck rims. Buster shambled around, mooching scratches and food wherever he found or could beg it.

China Grove wasn't a big town, so everybody knew everybody. Except for the Maryland boys. The Deuce drew lots of attention.

157

The band kicked off their first song, a Ray Charles.

Hey mama, don't you treat me wrong
Come and love your daddy all night long
All right now, hey hey, all right

Tad and Tom were listening to the band when a tall, stringy guy in jeans and a western shirt with fake pearl buttons came over. He wore cowboy boots, a Buck hunting knife hung from his belt. His straight black hair hung over his collar.

"Hey Tad, I ain't seen the band before, where they from?"

"They're out of Charlotte. Damn good, ain't they."

"I guess. The piano player's good for a nigger."

"Hey Jake, don't be like that. He's here to play music, not marry your sister."

"Keep my sister out of it!"

"I didn't mean nothin' by it."

Tad walked over to the cooler with Tom. "I shouldn't a mentioned his damn sister. She's not what you'd call picky, she's fucked every guy in town."

Ernie was leaning on the Deuce when the band took their first break.

"Wow, that's one nice car. Where'd you get it?"

It was the band's girl drummer. Brown-skinned, maybe eighteen, she was wearing jeans and a green blouse. She'd worked up a sweat on the drums, it soaked the blouse's armpits. Braids were rowed on the top of her head. Little beads trickled down from the tight curls on her forehead into her eyebrows. Pretty. Then Ernie saw her eyes.

In the darkness, the pupils were great dark wells, rimmed with green fire shot through with yellow streaks. When she blinked, she blinked slowly.

My god, she's beautiful.

He could barely speak.

He stammered, "Uh, down in Rock Hill."

"Well, it sure is pretty. Looks fast too."

"It's not very fast at this point. Doesn't have a motor."

"You gonna fix that?"

"That's the plan. We're taking it up to Maryland, I'll try and find a motor there. Something with power, maybe a hemi."

"What's a hemi?"

Ernie explained the legendary hemi, Chrysler's powerful V-8 with hemispherical combustion chambers.

"I love your band's music. Does the band bein' mixed, y'know, with colored and white players, cause hassles down here?"

"Sometimes. There's places that book us and places that don't. That's just the way it is. And sometimes we get some nasty comments from jerks in the audience. We just ignore 'em. You live in Maryland?"

"Yeah but I used to live down here, near Rock Hill. We moved when I was in sixth grade."

"How come you moved?"

"Well, partly because I was taking a lot of shit in school. You know, stuff like 'nigger hair.' And my mom found a job she really likes in Frederick, she's in charge of snakes and stuff at a funky zoo there."

"Snakes?"

"Yeah, and alligators and other stuff. She's a herpetologist."

"Is the race stuff better up there?"

"Yeah. It doesn't matter so much there. I mean, there's still stuff, but it's not so constant and so obvious. What're you doin' besides playin' music?

"I'm taking classes at Friendship Junior College in Rock Hill, my brother Harry is too. Is that your guitar sittin' on the front seat?"

"Yup."

"What do you do on it, what kinda music?"

"Basically rock, but most of what I do's really blues, just updated from when Black players did it in the old days. Stuff from Little Richard, Muddy Waters, Leadbelly, guys like that."

"Leadbelly! You do Leadbelly?"

"Yeah, a couple of his."

"You do 'How Long Blues'?"

"Well, yeah, I do."

"Yo Caroline!" The keyboard player waved at her.

"That's Harry, guess the break's over. Tell you what, would you like to sit in for a couple of songs next set?"

"I dunno. I'm not near as good as you guys."

"So you hit a couple wrong notes, what's the big deal? It's not like a final exam at music school."

"Okay. But you gotta promise you won't laugh."

"Promise I won't laugh. I'll ask Harry about it." She turned toward the band.

"Hey, did I hear your name right? Caroline?"

She nodded.

"Ernie."

Ernie was transfixed. He listened to every song, and his eyes never left Caroline.

> *How strange a trip this is. The radiator craps out, this nice guy appears from nowhere to fix it, takes us in, and now this amazing girl! I'd pinch myself, but I hear the music loud and clear, I'm not dreaming. Tho she sure is a dream.*

As the second set came to a close, Tom came over. "You should close your mouth, boy, you're doin' everything but drool!"

"Ah shut up."

"She sure is pretty. And she's comin' back."

Caroline was indeed walking back.

160

"Tell you what, I'll get outta your way." Tom headed to a cluster of guys by the Harley.

Caroline settled alongside Ernie against the Deuce.

"I talked to Harry, he says sure, it'd be fine if you sit in for a couple of songs next set. You still likin' our music?"

"It's flat-out great. And you're keepin' the band together, rock-solid on those skins. Y'know, you're the first girl drummer I've ever seen."

"You're right, it's weird, you'd think there's something about drumming that girls just can't do. Or don't do. Well, I can, and I do!"

"How'd you get into it?"

"Well, I actually grew up playin' flute, but there's not much call for flute in rock'n'roll. But Harry's been in bands since he was fifteen. I went to lots of his gigs, and sometimes between sets I sat down and messed around on the drums. And when the band left their gear at our house after practice, I'd mess around on 'em with records playing, copying riffs from Little Richard, Bo Diddley, Buddy Holly, Elvis, Jerry Lee. Turns out I'm a natural. A year ago his regular drummer went off to college, Berkelee Music in Boston, and the drum slot was empty. It wasn't empty long.

"Times are changing. More and more gals are playing, not just fronting a band like in the old days. Shit, one of the best bass players around is Carol Kaye, she's been a studio musician since the 50s. People are realizing, tits don't keep you from playin' an instrument."

"Are you guys planning on doin' this seriously, like making a record or something?"

"We talked about it, but all the big record companies are in New York or out in California. Charlotte definitely ain't the center of the record business. So I don't think so. We'll just keep on like we are, playing one or two nights a week. Finishing college is a lot more reliable way of making a living."

The band kicked off the third set with Jerry Lee Lewis' "Great Balls of

Fire," which got the crowd up dancing.

Then Harry introduced Ernie.

"Okay, we're gonna slow it down just a little bit. We got a Rock Hill boy here, moved up north, now he's back down south, gonna do a coupla blues songs, songs with Southern roots. Make Ernie Horton welcome to China Grove!"

By this time the beer had kicked in, and Ernie's acoustic songs didn't get much attention. A couple of polite claps. But he played okay, no big screwups. True to her word, Caroline didn't laugh. Most of the partygoers were lost in talk, flirting, bragging. Some were good and drunk. Ernie had just finished Little Richard's "I Hear you Knockin" when he heard yelling from a group over by the shop.

"Ain't no fuckin' Yankee gonna come down here and tell me what to say!"

Ernie saw someone waving his arms at another tall guy, Ernie couldn't tell who. He put the guitar down, walked toward the group. It was Jake, swinging at Mal. Mal had his arms up, bent with palms out, backing away.

Jake was pretty drunk. He kept coming. "Think you're fuckin' tough, do ya? You ain't tough, you're just fuckin' stupid." His punches were hitting Mal's arms.

Mal said, "Hey, man, I don't wanna fight. C'mon, this is a party, not a fight."

His entreaty did nothing. Jake kept punching, Mal kept backing, catching the blows on his forearms. He tripped over a car bench seat, fell, and Jake kicked him in the head. Mal scrambled to his feet. The cowboy boot had torn a gash in his forehead.

"Okay, if that's the way it's gonna be, you prick!"

He hit Jake twice, once in the gut, then, when he bent in pain, on the side of the face, and he went down. He lay curled, panting, spittle drooling from his mouth. The crowd around the boys was silent. Ernie elbowed through it.

"Mal, whaddya say we get out of here for awhile, maybe take

a run around the block? Maybe a bunch of blocks?"

"Yeah, that's probably a good idea. Give everybody a chance to cool down, sober up a bit." They walked to the Chrysler, which was parked over by the Deuce.

Ernie got into the driver's seat. Mal opened the passenger door, started to get in, then stopped, leaning into the car. "Maybe we ought to get Tom too. I 'spect we're not real popular with some of the, AHHHH!"

Jake's knife slashed between two of Mal's ribs on his right side. Mal fell face-forward onto the seat. "Shit!" He turned, tried to sit up.

Jake yelled, "You son of a bitch, how's that feel, asshole."

Mal wrenched himself up, grabbed Jake's arm and kicked him in the balls. Jake bent double. He smashed him in the jaw. He fell. Mal stood over him, swaying, "Oh shit, oh shit!"

Caroline ran to the Chrysler. The knife was sticking out of Mal's chest, blood streamed over his shirt."A doctor, a doctor, we've gotta get him to a doctor!"

Ernie muttered, "Mal, we gotta get you to a hospital?"

Tom held Mal's arm and eased him back into the passenger seat. "Don't touch that damn knife, it'll bleed even worse."

He slammed the passenger door. He and Caroline got in the back. Ernie started the Chrysler, swung it around and roared down the driveway. "Caroline, where's a damn hospital?"

"Charlotte."

"Shit, that's twenty miles away."

"That the closest there is."

He swung onto Route 29 and put the gas pedal to the floor. "Mal, how're you doin'?"

Mal groaned. "Not so good. Kinda dizzy."

"You're gonna be okay, we'll be at the hospital in no time, you're gonna be okay."

Despite the best efforts of the staff at the emergency room, Mal was not okay. A major vein was severed; he'd bled to death. The Charlotte police took Caroline, Tom and Ernie to the station, where they related the evening's events. The cops sent a car to Tad's to interview the partygoers.

A second car took Caroline and the two boys back to the hospital. One in the morning, they sat in the empty reception area of the ER.

Ernie shook his head. "I can't believe it. It just can't be real, why the hell did this happen?"

Tears running down her cheeks, Caroline took his hand. "It's dumb, it's just horrible dumb."

"I guess I've gotta call his father. Oh god, what's he gonna say?"

"Maybe the doctors here can help." Caroline went to the desk. One of the nurses called the doctor who'd been in charge of the resuscitation effort and he said he'd talk to Mal's father. But Ernie had to talk to him first.

Ernie leaned on the ER counter as he called Mal's home. The phone rang and rang, then Mal's father picked up. "Who is this?"

"Mister Alexopoulos, this is Ernie Horton."

"Ernie?"

"Yes sir."

"So what is it? I assume you're not calling me at half past one to tell me how good the Carolina weather is."

"No sir. There's some awful news."

He told him what had happened. Mal's father was stunned, then furious. Ernie passed the phone to the doctor, who relayed the medical details, told Mister Alexopoulos everything possible had been done for Mal and what had to happen next. Since it was clear a crime had happened, an autopsy. Mal's body would have to stay in the morgue until the police had completed whatever part of the investigation might require it. Then he could arrange to have an undertaker pick it up.

He gave the phone back to Ernie.

"I'm so, so sorry sir."

"You're sorry? I'm sorry, I'm sorry Mal ever met you and got involved with that damn car of yours!"

He hung up.

In silence, the band packed their gear in Harry's battered van. He drove the guitarist and horn player home, then went to the hospital. He and Caroline and the two boys sat on benches in the corner of the ER waiting room.

"I guess you guys are gonna be heading back to Maryland?" said Harry.

Tom answered, "Yeah, I guess. There's not a damn thing we can do for Mal, that's for sure. I wanna be outta this place."

"I feel the same way. Wish I'd never seen that damn Deuce." Ernie said.

Caroline squeezed his hand.

Tom had moved the Chrysler to the hospital parking lot. He got in the driver's seat. Ernie opened the passenger door. Mal's blood pooled on the floor, lay sticky on the seatcover, the car door, splashed on the glove compartment.

"Oh, Jesus." He shut the door, stood staring at the ground, arms limp by his sides.

Caroline took his hand, reached around him and hugged his back. "I'm so, so sorry. Could you call me when you get back to Maryland?"

"I'll call you."

She pulled a scrap of paper from her purse, wrote on it. "Here's my number."

Tom got in the driver's seat, Ernie got in the back. Caroline and her brother walked slowly to Harry's van. They all drove away from the hospital.

It was after noon when the sound of the Chrysler starting rumbled into Ernie's awareness. He sat up on his air mattress, saw Tad slam the hood. Tom had been sleeping on the Deuce's seat, he and Ernie went to the Chrysler.

"Man oh man, I'm so sorry about last night, Ernie, that fuckin' Jake, he's just a total asshole, a throwback. But there's no way I coulda kept him outta here. The cops came by, I think they've got him in jail."

"Asshole is right. Murderer."

"Yeah, yeah. I'm really sorry.

Well, your car's ready to go, the radiator's doin' its job. I cleaned most of the blood off the floor and the seat, but there's still some."

"Thanks."

"I don't know that I'm ever gonna have another party."

Tom paid Tad. They hitched the Deuce to the Chrysler and left.

The trip was long. Not long in time, or in mileage, the space between Buckeystown and Carolina was the same going back as it had been coming down. And the new radiator did its job, no stopping for water.

It was the silence. The stain and the smell of Mal's blood on the seatcover. The vacancy where he'd been sitting. The long, slow silence.

They were nearly in Virginia before Ernie said anything.

"I can't believe it, Tom. Mal's gone. His body's lying in the fucking morgue, cold and stiff and dead. I just can't believe it."

Tom stared through the rain-spattered windshield. "I can't either."

Ernie looked back at the Deuce, rain bouncing off its covering tarp.

166

"I wish I'd never seen that damn car."

They drove straight through, trading off driving, and pulled up at the farmhouse a little after midnight. They unhooked the Deuce from Tom's car and rolled it onto the grass alongside the barn.

Buckeystown

The next morning Ernie sat with his mom and dad at the breakfast table and gave them the grim details of the trip.

Della said, "My god, Mal's dead, stabbed to death. And he got killed because he didn't like that fella calling someone in the band nigger?"

"Yeah. You know how it is down there. Most of the kids at the party were okay, but that fella Jake's a complete asshole."

Ernest nodded. "There are still plenty of them down there. It's changing, but not very fast."

Della shook her head. "It's awful, just awful. I thank God you're okay, it coulda been you got stabbed. Now I sure regret us sending you down south to school, it's not like we didn't know Rock Hill.".

"What're your plans now? Do you want to go back to school somewhere?" Ernest asked.

"I oughta get a job. I need to start payin' you back what you loaned me."

"If you want to go back to school, we could let that debt slide."

"I may go back to school sometime, but not now. I'm gonna get a job."

Della said, "What about this gal Caroline? Sounds like you really like her."

"Yeah, I do. And I think she feels the same way."

Della and Ernest left for work. Ernie went out to the Deuce, pulled the tarp back. The paint still glistened, the engine compartment

167

still an emptiness waiting for a hemi. It wasn't going anywhere without an engine.

No, it's not going anywhere. Mal's sure not going anywhere. Where the hell am I going?

Images rolled through his mind. Mal's blood sticky on the Chrysler's floor. Mal's blood on his arm at the river.

If it wasn't for this fucking car Mal would still be here.

That evening he called Caroline. They talked for an hour.

Ernie took a job pumping gas at a Frederick Esso station, riding his bike to work each day. Phil, the owner, was a car nut, had several restored antiques. When Ernie told him about the Deuce they went to see it.

"Man, this is as classic as cars get. You did a great job on the interior and the paint, what're you gonna do for an engine?"

"I don't really know. I had plans, but now I, I just don't know. I used to see it with a hemi, clear as day, ready to roll and roar, but I just don't see that anymore."

"You wanna sell it?"

"Maybe. Let me think about it."

The next day he sold Phil the Deuce for $2000. The money went to his dad, repaying some of what he owed him. But not all. He figured another two or three months pumping gas would do it.

He called Caroline every week. They talked about music, about the band, about Mal, about being apart. She and Harry had joined the Friendly Student Civic Committee, a group at Friendship Junior College which was challenging segregated public facilities in Rock Hill and getting training in nonviolent protest techniques. The philosophy behind it had worked spectacularly for Gandhi as he banished the English from India, and had been adopted by the U.S. civil rights movement.

168

Jake Sharper was charged with second degree murder. His trial was scheduled in Charlotte for the beginning of November, and Ernie'd been called to testify. He dreaded reliving the pain of Mal's murder, but perhaps getting what was inside him out, and hopefully seeing that bastard sent to prison, would help.

As dreadful as that was, knowing he'd be with Caroline overwhelmed it.

January 9, 1961

A gentle snow had blanketed Buckeystown during the night. Final flakes drifted outside the window as Ernie and Tom sat in the farmhouse kitchen. With Della and Ernest at work, they talked alone.

Tom said, "So it's tomorrow you're goin' back for Sharper's trial?"

"Yeah, I'm takin' a bus tomorrow night. Any chance you could get me to the station?"

"What time?"

"Pretty late, think it's about 10 in the evening."

"Sure, no problem. Long as this snow doesn't get too deep. You gonna see Caroline?"

"Of course. How's school goin'?"

"Good I guess. My grades are good, I'm plannin' on transferring to a four-year school when Spring semester's over, probably University of Maryland in College Park. If we can afford it. How about you, any thoughts about goin' back to school?"

"Probably not, at least not now. There's just so much goin' on. Caroline of course, and that damn trial Wednesday. And I've gotta keep workin' at the station when I get back, at least till I can pay Dad back."

"How much d'you owe him?"

"I paid him some when I sold the Deuce, but it's still about two thousand bucks."

169

"Yeah, it does sound like you're life's kinda planned out for awhile."

"At least the next three or four months. After that, who knows. Caroline and Harry have been doin' civil rights stuff with other kids from Friendship Junior College, where they go. She wants me to go to some of the training classes they've been goin' to."

"You gonna?"

"I 'spect so."

At 9:30 the next evening Tom and Ernie stood next to a Greyhound bus at the Frederick station. The day had warmed. Yesterday's snow was slush under the bus's wheels.

Tom said, "So, guess it's goodbye again. Been a lotta them lately."

"Yeah, I guess. But look at it this way, any goodbye means a good hello somewhere down the line."

"I hope it's not too far down the line. Maybe one good summer day we'll be out on a rock in the Monocacy again with fishin' poles."

"Sounds great. I'll look forward to it."

"Goodbye, blood brother."

"The same to you, my friend."

As the bus rolled south through the night, Ernie thought of the words he might say when he testified, what he'd seen that awful day. He wasn't looking forward to it. But soon, soon there would be Caroline. Phone calls were better than nothing, but it sure wasn't like being with her. He longed to hear her real voice, warm and full without long distance static. See her face, those eyes. He still felt the warmth of her hug.

Soon was not very soon. He dozed, waking with his head leaning on the frigid window. Miles and miles of southern countryside, towns big and small slid by. One of the smallest, near Danville by Virginia's southern border. Tight Squeeze.

Oh yes. Caroline.

Two the next afternoon the bus pulled into Rock Hill. Through the window, there she was, arms crossed over a brown jacket that held off the winter chill. Her braids were gone, curls now bursting from her head, a burgeoning Afro framing her brown face. From that black and brown frame shone those sparkling green eyes.

He pulled his battered suitcase from the overhead, got off the bus. She said nothing, just ran to him, wrapped him in her arms and kissed him. For the very first time.

"Oh god, it's so good to see you!"

Again, words escaped Ernie. He dropped the suitcase, pulled her tight against him, buried his fingers in her curls. They stayed like that a long time, oblivious to the disdainful glances of the bus driver and some of the white passengers.

Ernie said, "Y'know, we can't stay like this forever."

"Mmmm, but it feels so good, so good."

They unwound themselves and started walking to Caroline's house. Now at Friendship Junior College full-time, Caroline had moved from her parents' Charlotte rowhouse to a small house on Roddy Street in Rock Hill which she shared with 3 other girls. As they walked, she told him more about the Student Committee and the nonviolence training they were getting from James McCain and Tom Gaither, field directors for CORE, the Congress of Racial Equality.

Raised near Winnsboro, Gaither was a veteran of sit-ins at Orangeburg and Greensboro. Although there had been demonstrations in Rock Hill—sit-ins at the Woolworth's and McCrory's lunch counters—they'd been comparatively spontaneous, and the participants had received little or no training.

Ernie sat on the couch as Caroline made sandwiches.

"There's actually gonna be training sessions this week, probably every day. Harry and I've been going to them. You wanna go to one?"

171

"Yeah, maybe. Depends when this trial gets done."

"That probably wouldn't interfere, the sessions are in the evening."

She described the brutally realistic training.

"We break up into teams, one playing the role of the folks sittin' in, the other the attackers. The sitters-in are in chairs, like you'd be if you were at a lunch counter. The attackers do all sorts of nasty shit, blow smoke in your face, say things like 'nigger, you're so black you make this whole room dark! We gonna send you back to Africa, jungle bunny!' And they shove you and pinch you and throw stuff like flour and sugar and water on you. You sure don't wanna be wearing good clothes at the training. But when you do it for real, you do."

"Damn, that sounds tough!"

"Then the teams swap roles, the sitters attack and the attackers sit. The swapping's a good way to put distance between what's happening and what you're feeling. It reminds you that you're playing a role, a role that's a vital part of the movement. This is the way we fight back, with nonviolence.

"And if you're playin' the role of a white person, and you were raised like many white people in the south are raised, you could be the one saying that shit. Even if deep down you're actually a good person, those hateful words could be coming out of you."

"Not just words." Ernie was thinking of Sharper and the upcoming trial.

"Yeah, I know. It hurts, it hurts. Folks been hurtin' from that hate for a long time. And a lot of folks ended up the same way Mal did."

They sat in silence. Their sandwiches were finished. The sun had set.

Caroline laid the dishes in the sink. "Okay, sadness is here and it will always be part of who we are and what happens to us. But it doesn't have to crush us every damn minute."

She took his hand, pulled him off the couch, led him toward

172

the bedroom. "My roommate isn't here tonight, she's off seeing somebody."

Actually, Caroline had strongly suggested to her roommate Sarah—Sarah would have said demanded—that she find another bed that night. Maybe the rest of the week too.

The room was small, so was the bed, just a single bed. In which, for the first time, they made love. On a dresser, two candles flickered. His eyes watched hers as she drank him, enveloped him. So green, so open. Until ecstasy fluttered them closed.

Later, she fell asleep on him, her breast on his chest, her curls brushing his ear, vibrant pubic curls against his thigh. He lay awake a long time. The bed was not too small. He was happier than he could ever remember being.

Caroline woke before Ernie. She was alongside him now, her arm across his. Their colors. His, a tan-orange with brown freckles, hers a tan-brown, smooth, unfreckled. How wonderful that their love didn't care about that difference, knew just how small it was. And she knew that when folks looked at him, most of them saw White. He hadn't had to live with all the stuff that goes with being "black," he'd been "white."

The alarm jangled Ernie into awakeness at six. Caroline was on her side, looking at him.

Ernie rubbed his eyes. "Awake, huh? What're you doin' anyhow?"

"Just lookin' at you, love."

He stroked her smooth cheek, the sweet brown skin of her back. "God, you are so beautiful. Y'know, white girls lie in the sun for hours tryin' to get the color you got?"

"Yeah, I know, it's strange, ain't it. They put down colored folks, then blister their bellies tryin' to look like them. But you're not too bad-lookin' yourself, darlin'. I don't even mind you been passin' as a white boy."

"That ain't fair!" He pinched her bottom.

"Well, maybe it ain't. Actually, I'd say you done a lot better than just pass last night. I'm givin' you an A."

"You get A plus from me, lovely." He kissed her. "In fact, maybe we oughta take that exam over."

She sighed and frowned. "Lawd, would I love to, but you got some nasty shit on your plate this mornin'. We gotta get up, gotta be at the courthouse at nine. "

She flipped the covers off them, giggled when she saw his hard cock. "No, not THAT up, you gotta get your BUTT up and get dressed. We got a bus to catch in an hour."

He watched as she stood and walked to the closet for her wrap. Her every step was a gift for his eyes.

Toast popped from the toaster, Caroline put it on plates with butter and jelly.

"We jes' don't have time for bacon and eggs today."

They were at the bus station before seven and caught the seven-fifteen to Charlotte, arriving a little before eight. A blustery west wind chilled their faces as they walked, tight together, the eight blocks to the courthouse.

The courthouse was imposing, its three stories fronted with ten marble columns and broad marble steps. Caroline pointed at a pillar in front of the building. It looked like a miniature Washington Monument, twenty feet tall, brass plaques at its base.

"Some of the Mecklenburg County folks are convinced this county declared independence from England before any of the states did, that's what that monument's about. When my dad was a kid, there was even a state holiday in May called Meck Dec Day. There's some independent, stubborn folks in this part of the world."

They climbed the marble steps, entered the building through tall, heavy brass doors colored with patches of green weathering. Their steps echoed through the cavernous lobby, its high ceilings and

174

marble walls. A clerk at the information booth directed them to the first-floor courtroom for the Sharper trial.

They sat on a wooden bench outside the courtroom. A black felt board by the door read

Mecklenburg County Superior Court
January 11, 1961
9:00 am Criminal Trial, Hon. Richard Hatch presiding
Charge: Second-Degree Murder

"This is about the farthest thing from fun I could think of," Ernie said.

"Yeah I agree. But look at it this way, at least we're not on the top floor."

"Top floor?"

"There's actually four floors on this building, the top one is the jail. About twenty cells up there, a little flat-topped chunk, like a separate piece plopped on top of this fancy court. Down here we got air conditioning. Up there, forget it. You can imagine what those cells are like in a Carolina summer."

"How come you know so much about it?"

"Hey, I grew up here. I grew up colored here. Coupla friends who spent time in those cells, they ain't nice. You get arrested for a sit-in, a demonstration in this county, that's where you're gonna be. May not be as bad as hard labor at the York County prison or Parchman Farm, but it ain't nice."

Ernie Horton was the first witness called by the prosecution. He was sworn in and the prosecutor began by asking what had brought him to Tad's house in China Grove. Ernie explained the journey, its reasons, its problems. Leaving Winthrop, the radiator dying, Tad's stopping to help, his generosity. Tad suggesting they stay for the party. Staying.

"Mr. Horton, do you know what the basis of the disagreement

175

between the defendant and the deceased was?"

"No sir, I really don't. I wasn't near them when the argument started. I did hear Jake yell somethin' about 'damn Yankee.'"

"And then what happened?"

"I ran over there. Jake tried to hit Mal. Mal didn't really fight, he just held his arms up and backed away. But he tripped, and Jake kicked him in the head. Mal got up and hit Jake a couple of times, knocked him down. I told Mal the best thing for us to do would be to just leave. We went over to the car. He was getting in it when Jake stabbed him in the back, and then stabbed him in the chest."

The prosecutor walked to the jury bench and held up a bone-handled Buck knife and sheath.

"Doctors removed this knife from Malcolm Alexopoulos' chest at Charlotte Hospital on September 11 at approximately 10:30 pm. Resuscitation efforts were ineffective. Alexopoulos was pronounced dead at 11:22. It's the coroner's opinion, he'll confirm this later, that this knife was the cause of death. Charlotte police arrested Mr. Sharper later that night. The next day, police investigators found this sheath, which carries the imprint of this knife, in Mr. Sharper's trash."

The attorney excused Ernie from the witness stand and called Tad Custis.

"Mr. Custis, can you tell the jury the substance of the argument between the defendant and Mr. Alexopoulos that preceded the fight."

"I guess it was really about people's color. Jake was talking about the two black kids in the band, and about colored people in general. He was saying nigger a lot. Mal asked him why he was using that word, it was really hurtful. Jake said he didn't give a shit about hurting niggers and he wasn't gonna listen to, sorry for the language, judge, a fuckin' Yankee. That's how it got started."

"And then what happened?"

Tad's testimony was essentially a repetition of Ernie's. The defense attorney mounted what defense he could, calling two of

Sharper's friends to testify to his character. Their testimony was effectively rebutted by additional evidence the prosecution had submitted to the judge—Sharper's two prior assault convictions—though it wasn't clear whether the judge would allow that fact to be presented to the jury.

In the end, that didn't matter. The trial completed the next morning. Caroline and Ernie, now excused as a witness, were in the audience as the jury returned a verdict of guilty and recommended that Jake Sharper be imprisoned for ten years.

That evening they attended a training session led by CORE's James McCain. McCain explained some of the strategy behind the nonviolent campaign.

"Think about what it would be like to be in the shoes of the folks who're attacking you. They spit on you, slap you, spill food on you. But you don't react. You don't react! That's something they'll think about then, and even more when they look back on it. It won't be fast, but there will be change.

"The news media will spread the story. Some of them won't report it accurately, but some of them will. And anybody who calls himself a Christian will remember the Bible words, 'Turn the other cheek.'

"Doctor King summarized it well, he said 'Don't let them get you to hate them.' Everybody here feels deep down what we're doin'. It's time for a change, that's why we're here. Like Dr. King said, 'If you live and you don't have an impact on change, then your living is in vain.' But know your impact has a cost. You will be beaten and arrested."

At every sit-in, a team member who didn't plan to be arrested carried the phone numbers of local ambulance services.

As they walked back to Caroline's, she told him about the sit-ins Dr. King had been leading in Atlanta.

Ernie nodded, "Yeah, I saw him getting arrested on TV."

"Like Mr. McCain said, that's what you gotta expect. And like he said, the folks in the movement are ready for that. They're in this with their whole heart. I mean, it's not like some authority, the government or something, told you to go do this, get arrested and maybe put your life in danger."

"Yeah, I been thinkin' some about that. I just had to register for the draft, so now I'm not in school I could get drafted."

"Yup. And you don't have any choice about what the army does with you once you're in. They send you off to a war, it don't matter whether you think that war's right or wrong. They tell you what to do. You go, and you could die.

"What we're doin' is very different. There's some of the same dangers as a war, but it's a nonviolent war. Nobody else tells you to do it. Nobody tells you but you."

Though it was nearly midnight when they got back to Caroline's house, they weren't tired. They made love again and lay wrapped together.

Ernie ran his fingers over her cheek. "God, it's just so wonderful to finally be here with you. So wonderful it's hard to believe. And so hard to believe everything that's happened since we met. And even how we met!"

"Yeah, it is. It almost feels like some great power planned it. God?"

"I don't know about God. If he is real, and he did plan us, why the hell would he plan what happened to Mal?"

They lay in silence. Touched, stroked, looked.

"So what now, my love? You're going back tomorrow, right?"

"Yeah, I've gotta get back home. It was hard to get this time off from work with Phil, he's doing double duty at the station. And I've gotta keep that job, I still owe my dad money for the Winthrop tuition and what I spent getting the Deuce back home."

178

Well after midnight, wrapped together, they fell asleep and stayed asleep long after the sun rose. Ernie woke first. He felt the warmth of her breath on the side of his face. He stroked her beautiful brown breast. Those beautiful breasts that would nurse babies they might have. White babies. Brown babies. Does it matter?

Babies.

Eyes still closed, she smiled. Slowly she opened them, reached for his cock.

"Mmmm, mmm, I see you're ready."

They made love. Slowly. Very slowly. Afterwards, they lay side by side, eyes still making love.

"God, I love being inside you!"

"I love you there."

"I really mean being inside you, not just my cock, all of me. It's like I'm all enclosed by you, by your pussy, your arms, your love."

Caroline put her fingers on his lips. "That's so beautiful, my love, so beautiful. Yes, yes, I enfold you. All of you."

He kissed her fingers. "I want this to last forever."

She stroked his face. "I do too. But we have to eat or we won't last at all. You stay in bed, I'll get us some real breakfast."

As she headed for the kitchen the phone rang.

"Oh hello Mom."

The conversation was one-sided, long silences from Caroline as her mother talked. After five minutes or so, she said goodbye.

"Mom, yeah, we'll be careful. Thanks for callin'."

"Your mom, huh?"

"Yeah."

"Worried?"

"Yeah, she's concerned about me and Harry doing the sit-ins. The newspaper's been reporting them, the local Klan is mouthing off, and there's somethin' called the White Citizens' Council just had a meeting at the high school. They had about five hundred people there, callin' us rabble-rousers and communists. And Reverend Ivory, he's the head of the local NAACP chapter, found bullet holes in his front door when he got home last week. So yeah, she's worried."

Late that morning they walked to the Greyhound station, Ernie's arm over her shoulder, hers around his waist. A cold wind blew from the west. The sun warmed their faces. Hugging in front of the open bus door, their goodbyes.

"Wish you weren't goin', love. Wish you were gonna be back tomorrow."

"I sure wish it was gonna be tomorrow, but you know it can't be. I still owe my dad nearly two thousand bucks, figure it'll take two or three months. I gave him some of it when I sold Phil the Deuce. He put a sweet hemi in it, it's a lot more than just the pretty promise it was when I towed it up there."

"Mmm. Speakin' of pretty promises, you got one for me?"

"Yeah, pretty, I'll make you a promise. I promise to get my butt back to you just as fast as I can. And I want you to make me a promise too."

"Yeah, what?"

"That you're not gonna get hurt at a sit-in. I wish I could be there with you. At least I could stand in front of you if some asshole tries to smack you with a bottle or a brick or somethin'."

"I'll do my best. I'll watch out for assholes with bottles or bricks."

January 31, 1961

> *From the Associated Press:*
> *Ten Negro college students ignored the warning of South Carolina's chief law enforcement officer Tuesday and carried their anti-segregation demonstration to McCrory's lunch*

180

*counter. The 10, arrested for trespass,
entered jail singing hymns and patriotic
songs. The next day, 10 were convicted
of trespassing and breach of the peace
and sentenced to serve 30 days in jail or
to pay a $100 fine. One man paid a fine,
but the remaining nine—eight of whom
were Friendship Junior College
students—chose to take the sentence of
30 days hard labor at the York County
Prison Farm.*

With the exception of Tom Gaither, all the imprisoned demonstrators
were members of the Friendly Student Civic Committee. And all were
male. Caroline and her roommate Sarah had carried signs outside
McCrory's, but weren't arrested. At this point in the movement,
leaders were hesitant to put women in Southern jails.

This wasn't the first time Committee members had been
arrested, but this arrest marked a new phase in the movement. At a
Committee session before the sit-in, Gaither had outlined the strategy.

"In the past, when police arrest us and take us to jail they
charge us and everything, and they let us go. There's something else
we can do. We're going to refuse to leave. They lock us up, they're
going to have to deal with us."

Caroline raised her hand. "Some of the papers, and a lot of the
politicians, they're saying we're just a bunch of attention seekers
listening to rabble-rousers from out of state. How do we deal with that
if we're asked?"

"As far as out of state, you know the truth to that, just tell it.
Almost all you students are from Carolina. I am too. This is my state,
I was raised forty miles from here. And yes, folks will say we're
publicity hounds. It's certainly true that we're looking for publicity, it's
vital to the movement. When folks see a student who's done nothing

181

more criminal than carry a sign on a public street beaten with a club or knocked down by a firehose, it has an effect. Yeah, some cheer, like 'serves the bastard right,' but a whole lot don't cheer. Some of 'em see that violence is totally against their religion. Even if they're not religious, many of 'em will see it's just unfair. Yes, it is publicity, but it's publicity with a purpose. It's drama."

The students' decision to remain in prison was the beginning of the "Jail, No Bail" movement. Jail No Bail reduced the financial burden on CORE, simultaneously saddling the local government with the costs of imprisonment and feeding.

The notoriously tough Captain Dagler bossed the group during its stay at the Prison Farm. On the first day in prison, he tried to force Willy Massey to cut his goatee. "Boy, cut that thing from under your chin and pull off that jitterbug hat. You're on the chain gang now!"

Nine of the group were students, and had brought textbooks to the prison to keep up their studies. On their sixth day in jail, Dagler confiscated all the books, claiming the prison "didn't want to be responsible for them." When Gaither assured him the students would be responsible for their own books, Dagler responded he was "simply carrying out orders."

"Who gave the orders?" Gaither asked.

"Quit asking questions. This is a prison, not a damned school. If this was a school, we'd have teachers here, not guards."

At one point, the entire group was put in solitary confinement for singing the song, "Oh Freedom, Before I'd be a slave, I'd be buried in my grave." But even in solitary, they continued to sing, "Ain't Gonna Let Nobody Turn Me Round" echoed through the prison.

As further punishment, they were restricted to bread and water.

Reverend Cecil Ivory

Not all the protesters were jailed. Wary of bad publicity, the cops didn't arrest the girls, Caroline among them, who'd joined the demonstration. They came to be known as the "City Girls" since they all lived in Rock Hill.

Nor did they arrest NAACP president Cecil Ivory, who'd been protesting from his wheelchair. This protest was far from his first action against segregation. In 1957 he'd organized a boycott of the local bus company and established an alternative service comprising two buses purchased with community donations.

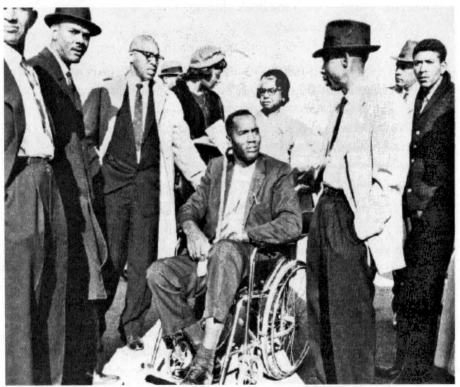

As on most southern buses in that era, despite Supreme Court decisions outlawing segregation on public transportation, Blacks were required to sit in the back. Many local and state laws ignored the Supreme Court, but increasingly those laws and customs were challenged. On July 13, 1957, Black maid Addelene Austin boarded a Star bus. The only empty seat was not in the back, it was next to a white woman, who gestured Austin to sit there. The driver refused to allow it. Furious, Austin got off the bus and walked home.

The boycott emptied Star Bus Line of Black riders. Despite the local Klan offering financial support, the company closed within a year.

Ivory's leadership extended far beyond organizing demonstrations. He wrote notes on the back of many of his bank deposit slips during this period, handing the slip to the bank teller — White, of course —with the back side up.

A typical note read:

> *We do not protest against you. We protest your evil and unjust system of segregation and discrimination. We will return your hate with love. We will endure your oppression with patience, but we will protest until death, if need be, your unjust policies.*

On February 12 and again the next week, Ivory led caravans of cars to the isolated prison farm, where he spoke to the Black and White visitors. A barbed-wire fence, newly erected by the farm's prisoners, kept the visitors from approaching the compound closely. Caroline, Sarah and Harry, in Harry's van, were part of the second caravan. As he drove to the prison, Harry raved about Reverend Ivory.

"He may be in a wheelchair, but he's a damn strong man. He was a great athlete in high school, played football and basketball, got an athletic scholarship to college. He would've been in prison with these guys, he was at McCrory's with them, but he wasn't able to raise up from his chair, so they didn't arrest him."

"Wow, he sounds like somethin' else," said Sarah.

Caroline had brought the Rock Hill and Columbia newspapers along and was scanning them for coverage of the demonstrations. "Listen to this, somethin' from an editorial.

"The invasion of York County by persons from other sections of the country for purpose of propaganda and the flaunting of the

laws and customs of South Carolina is another reflection of the irresponsible lawlessness which has developed over the segregation-integration issue."

Harry nodded, "Yup, that's us. Irresponsible propagandists."

Caroline continued, "And how about this, they're reporting what happened at the Rock Hill White Citizens Council meeting. Some preacher named McCord.

"'Segregation is morally right and theologically right. God made the white man, God made the black man. Who made the mulatto? He is the work of Satan. You cannot mistreat the Negro but you cannot allow him to be pushed on by godless communism to destroy our country. We are at war. It is a religious war between godless communism and christian America.'"

Harry shook his head. "Yup, tellin' it like it is, not just irresponsible propagandists, but immoral communists out to destroy Christianity. And he thinks Satan's been makin' mulatto kids, not white men? Gimme a break!"

"And there's this from Mr. Smith, the Council president.

"'Any minister who leads a sit-in, kneel-in, wade-in or any kind of an in is a sinner before God. How can a minister lead people to break the last commandment I do not understand. That commandment is 'Thou shalt not covet' and when they are leading these people in these kinds of acts they are teaching them to covet.'"

Sarah chuckled. "Teaching them to covet? What on earth does he think we're coveting? Is there something wrong with wanting to be recognized as full humans beings?"

"Guess so, at least in his bible."

When the students complete their sentences—they are the first to serve their entire sentence for a sit-in arrest— they're honored by a mass meeting at Emmet Scott School in Rock Hill, where Della had taught years ago. James Farmer of CORE spoke, as did soon-to-become SNCC field director Charles Sherrod. Sherrod described one

185

of the positive aspects of the prison experience.

"You get ideas in jail. You talk with other young people you have never seen. Right away we recognize each other. People like yourself, getting out of the past. We're up all night, sharing creativity, planning action. You learn the truth in prison, you learn wholeness. You find out the difference between being dead and alive.

"And you find solidarity across the color line sometimes. Some of the jailers sure weren't happy to see a few of the White prisoners singing songs like 'Ain't Gonna Let Nobody Turn Me Round' with us."

Demonstrations continued in Rock Hill and spread across the state through the Spring. Spearheaded by the local Ku Klux Klan, the response was often violent. White students erected a ten-foot wooden cross on the Winthrop campus one night and set it afire. Interviewed by the local paper, Sheriff "Tank" Rogers downplayed the incident.

"Just a couple of kids workin' off the stress of finals."

The Freedom Rides

May 2, 1961

Washington, D.C.

Eating places were not the only public facilities where segregation was directly challenged. On May 2, twelve black and white trainees, future Congressman John Lewis among them, are welcomed by CORE's James Farmer at the Quaker Fellowship House in Washington, DC. They undergo three days of intense training in preparation for bus trips intended to demonstrate the validity of the Supreme Court decision declaring

186

segregation on interstate transport unconstitutional. After training, the Riders are split into two teams, one to travel on Greyhound lines, the other on Trailways, starting in Washington and ending in New Orleans with multiple stops between. As with sit-in training, the danger to participants is not minimized. They are advised to write their final will and testament, perhaps also a eulogy, before they leave.

May 8, 1961

Late in the afternoon, Ernie again talked with Caroline on the phone. His father's paid off and there's enough money in his pocket to get started in Rock Hill. Soon, soon they'd be together, and not just for a visit of a few days. One of the girls in her house has moved out, so there's room for him. In her room. In her bed.

"I can't hardly say how much I'm missing you, Caroline. God, it's been almost five months, I'm about goin' crazy."

"You're not the only one goin' crazy, love. Crazy with love. And I've got a surprise for you."

"A surprise?"

"Yeah, a surprise."

"Hey, that's not fair. Couldn't you at least give me a little hint?" Caroline was quiet a few seconds.

"Okay, a hint. It's very personal. And very loving."

At 8 that evening, Ernie got into his dad's car. He'd had a long talk with his parents about the trip. They supported his reasoning, but were anxious. Terribly anxious.

His dad got into the driver's seat.

"Son, please, please be careful. And call us, let us know what's

187

happening down there. We don't want some Rock Hill cop calling us saying you're lying in the hospital. Or worse."

"I'll call, I promise. And I won't take any unnecessary chances."

"I don't know what to call necessary and what to call unnecessary. If you go to demonstrations with Caroline, you're both taking a chance. It's South Carolina, not Maryland. I know the difference first hand."

"I know. We'll be careful. And I'll call."

They pulled into the Frederick Greyhound station. Ernie got his bags out of the trunk and set them down. His dad hugged him.

"I love you. I'm proud of you. Call."

The bus pulled into Washington close to midnight. Union Station was empty, cavernous and cold. He put his bag in a locker and stepped out into the Spring air.

The city's bustle was slowed. A few cabs waited in front of the station. To the south, the Capitol's dome gleamed. Farther away the pointed pillar of the Washington Monument shone white. Ernie went back in the station, stretched out on a hard wooden bench, jacket rolled under his head, and slept fitfully.

At seven the next morning, he boarded the bus for Rock Hill. As he gave his bags to the new driver, he had no idea what a ride he was in for.

Five well-dressed Black men boarded at Charlotte, North Carolina. Among the Freedom Riders was future congressman John Lewis.

FBI bulletins had briefed local police departments on the Riders' route and schedule. With these details, some departments, many of whom were Klan members, planned a reception for the Riders. The FBI was fully aware of the Klan's plans. Gary Rowe, a member of Eastview Klavern but also a paid informant, had reported Cook's instructions, but the FBI did nothing.

In Birmingham, Sergeant Tom Cook told members of Eastview Klavern 13, the most violent Klan chapter, "We're gonna allow you fifteen minutes....You can beat 'em, bomb 'em, maim 'em, kill 'em. I don't give a shit. There will be absolutely no arrests. You can assure every Klansman in the country that no one will be arrested in Alabama for that fifteen minutes."

In Rock Hill, Bobby Rogers, the sheriff's brother, prepared local Klansmen for the Ride's arrival at the Greyhound station.

"The race-mixing bastards are gonna get here around 3 Tuesday. Get there at 2:00 and be ready. Tank says he'll have a couple of deputies there, but they won't do a damn thing till we've showed 'em how we feel."

When the bus arrived shortly after 3:00, Bobby, Elwin Wilson, and ten other Klansmen were waiting. Bag in hand, Ernie walked into the bus station, and was behind John Lewis as he walked toward the rest room with its WHITE sign.

Bobby stepped in front of Lewis. "Other side, nigger," he said, pointing down the hall to a door with its COLORED sign.

Lewis looked directly at Wilson. "I have a right to go in there. The Supreme Court has guaranteed that right."

"Shit on that," said Bobby.

Wilson hit Lewis on the back of his head with brass knuckles, knocking him against the tiled station wall. Al Bigelow, one of the other Riders, stepped between Lewis and the Klan group, arms at his sides as the Riders' non-violent training had taught. An ax handle dropped him to his knees, then to the floor.

Genevieve Hughes, the only white woman in the Riders, was also knocked down. As Ernie bent to help her a brass-knuckled fist smashed his cheek and he fell. The Klan group kicked the fallen men. Blood smeared the wall and pooled on the floor.

Ernie staggered to his feet, blood dripping from his cheek as the two deputies, who'd been inside the waiting room, burst out. "OK boys, that's enough, that's enough." The Klansmen backed away from

189

the Riders toward the station door, one spitting at the group as he left. Lewis leaned against the wall, blood streaming from cuts around his eyes and mouth.

Hughes, bleeding herself, brought wet paper towels from the bathroom and wiped Lewis' cuts.

"Are you OK, John?"

"My ribs hurt, but I don't think there's anything broken. Take care of those other fellows."

She wiped Ernie's face. "How'd you get involved in this, young man? We came here knowing there was danger, but why you?"

"I didn't know when I got on the bus, but I do now. This is a Freedom Ride, isn't it?"

"Yes, it is."

A police officer approached the little group huddled in the hallway and spoke to Lewis. "Do you want to press charges against the guys who attacked you?"

Surprised, Lewis looked up at the officer through a rapidly closing eye. "No, no, we won't be pressing charges."

Five minutes later, Caroline and her roommate Sarah burst through the door and saw Ernie. "Oh my god, look at you! Are you alright?"

Aware that the Freedom Ride was scheduled to stop at Rock Hill, the Friendly Student Committee had planned to greet the Riders, but had been stuck in traffic. Until this minute, Caroline hadn't realized Ernie was on the same bus. Gladys, another of the City Girls, fetched a first aid kit from her car. She, Caroline and Hughes finished cleaning the group's wounds and put bandages on. John Lewis and the other Riders went into the station restaurant and ordered cups of coffee. Very hard-earned coffee.

Back at Caroline's house, Ernie sat on the couch, marveling at the coincidence that had put him on the same bus as the Riders. "It's hard to believe. Just comin' down to you, and look what happens.

190

You're a damn Freedom Rider!

"Sometimes you gotta wonder if fate has your life planned out for you. But I'm so glad you're not worse hurt. Let me take a look at that cut."

She pulled the bandage off. "Well, it's bruised, but the cut isn't too bad, don't think we need to get you stitched. And it's stopped bleeding."

"Glad to hear I'm not dyin'. If I did I'd never get to know about that surprise you got for me. Remember, that personal surprise? I maybe got hit on the head, but not hard enough to make me forget that."

Caroline raised her eyebrows. "Oh yeah. But I dunno whether a beat-up boy's up for that lovin' surprise."

"I'm not that beat-up. And it's been a long, long time."

Caroline reached out a hand and led Ernie back to the bedroom. She pulled the window shades down.

"Why don't you light the candles on the dresser?"

As Ernie lit the candles, she pulled her blouse over her head, unfastened her bra, slid her shoes off and pulled her slacks down. Only her underpants were left as she sat on the edge of the bed.

She grinned. "Okay, come here, just kneel here by the bed."

As he kneeled she lay back and raised her hips.

"Pull 'em off."

He clenched the edges of her underpants and pulled them slowly down her legs.

"Oh my. Oh my."

The tight curls of her pubic hair had been shaved into a heart. The two curls at the top of the heart met at the top of her vagina.

"Can I kiss your heart?"

"It's all yours. All of me is all yours."

He bent, fondled her curls with his nose, smelled her deliciousness. He turned his head slowly, brushing her with his cheeks and lips. He kissed her.

191

She groaned in delight. "Oh my love, my love!"

While Ernie and Caroline sharing their hearts—both symbolic and curly—the second Freedom Ride bus pulled into the Rock Hill Trailways station. Aware of the earlier violence, Trailways had closed and locked the station, but it was surrounded with cars and people, some screaming at the Riders as they got off the bus.

Not all the crowd was belligerent. Among it was half a dozen cars, a transport squad organized by Reverend Ivory. As the Riders hurried into the cars, from his wheelchair Ivory stared without flinching at the mob lining the other side of the street.

"Coon!"

"Black nigger!"

"Get the hell out of town!"

A dozen cars, spouting epithets and middle fingers, followed the squad as it drove from the station to Ivory's home, where his wife Emily served everybody supper.

The rest of May was as close to heaven as Ernie had ever experienced. These weeks were the longest continuous time he and Caroline had been together, and they were together virtually every minute except when she was attending class. Two evenings they attended CORE training sessions, preparing for the next Rock Hill sit-in.

They spent four balmy days in the city's parks. Many days and nights were spent exploring each other in every way, discovering, discovering. Exploring their love.

June 2, 1961

The alarm clock went off at 5:30. Ernie and Caroline dressed, she in a flowered dress, he in slacks and a button-down shirt. He fumbled with his tie, his only tie.

"Here, let me help you."

She stood behind him, reached around to tie the tie. Her

192

breasts pressed against his back,

Ernie leaned back into her. "Mmm, guess I should wear ties more often. I'm no good at tying 'em, will you always do it for me?"

"C'mon, 'nuffa that, we gotta get serious."

She stepped in front of him, smoothed the knot. "There, you're lookin' good."

They sat at the breakfast table eating toast and jelly.

Caroline sipped coffee. "So my love, you're 'bout to break your protest cherry!"

Ernie grinned. "That's the plan."

"Lookin' forward to your first time?"

"I guess."

"Little scared?"

"Yeah. But excited too. It's been comin' a long time."

"I'll be right there with you. And our friends from the Committee."

When McCrory's opened at 7, eight members of the Friendly Student Committee stepped through the door and went straight to the unoccupied lunch counter. Tying on her white apron, a waitress saw them through the swinging kitchen door.

She yelled back to the cook, "Art, they're here again. Those damn niggers are here. There's a white boy with 'em this time."

The cook pushed the door open. "Dammit. We won't sell shit as long as they're here."

The students filled all but one of the counter's stools. Ernie slid a plastic-framed menu from the back of the counter and studied it in the tense silence, hands shaking.

Caroline leaned to him, whispered, "You want pie with your coffee, or maybe a coupla donuts?"

He shook his head, restrained a giggle.

Art picked up the phone and dialed. "I'll get 'em outta here."

Fifteen minutes later, five cars pulled up and parked against the curb in front of McCrory's. A dozen white boys, none older than mid-twenties, got out. Sarah and Gladys were walking the sidewalk in front of the store, holding cardboard posters in front of them.

Can't Eat
Don't Buy

Three of the boys stepped in front of Sarah, blocking her. One pulled a cigarette out, lit it and threw the match, still burning, onto her shoe. She snuffed the flame with her other foot.

He sneered, "I'm gonna eat and I'm gonna buy, bitch." He spat on her sign. The rest of the group ignored her as they brushed past into the narrow lunchroom.

The room echoed with insults as the boys arrayed behind the students at the counter.

"Get outta here, nigger, you're makin' this whole room black!"

" Get back to Africa, jungle bunny!"

One poked at Ernie's head. "You call that hair, boy? Looks like a dirty sheep's ass to me!"

Ernie was amazed at how closely their words and actions echoed the training they'd gone through with James McCain. One pulled a glass sugar container from the counter, screwed the top off and poured it over Ernie's head. Another blew cigarette smoke in his face. A third poured a glass of water over Caroline's head and shoulders, soaking her hair.

Out of the corner of her eye, Caroline saw Ernie lean back, take a deep breath and hold it. She reached over, held his arm and whispered "My love. My love."

He looked at her, she turned her face to him. Wet hair stuck to her cheeks but the corners of her mouth turned up in a little smile. Above it, her eyes still shone. Green, green.

He let the breath out, bent his head and sat.

Sat in.

****

Note

The newspaper articles on pages 111 and 112 are not actually from the "Charlotte Clarion," they're verbatim from the Norfolk Landmark. Fletcher was lynched a mile and a half north of the Accomack County, Virginia courthouse, ten miles from where I live.

Epilogue

Photo credit: Jeremi Galpin

As I wrote the story you just read, well into the ninth decade of my life, the fourth of my great-grandchildren was born. The two oldest, Gabriel Beard (right) and Maddox Galpin-Shores are above.

Age does give perspective, and part of the perspective that hammered home to me as I researched and wrote is that our civil war was recent. Not yesterday, but pretty damn recent. Its last veteran, Albert Woolson, died in August of 1956, 109 years old. I was 15. Considering only age, he could have been my grandfather, could have told me his war tales around the dinner table. My great-grandparents, born in the 1830s and 1840s, were alive when that war was fought. They read in their British newspapers of the rent in America's fabric, the stories of catastrophic death and destruction in this country.

It was catastrophic on a scale Americans alive today haven't experienced. We lament the losses in the wars we remember: friends, uncles, fathers—now mothers, sisters and aunts—dead or crippled. But the scale of loss that fell on the South, to a lesser extent on the North, during our civil war is beyond anything in our memory.

58,220 Americans died in the Vietnam war; 0.03% of our population. Ten times that percentage, about 400,000, 0.31% of our population, died in World War II. **Seventeen times** that World War II percentage, about 290,000 Confederate combatants, died during our civil war. That's 5.3% of the South's White population. (It's appropriate to limit the population to Whites because almost no Blacks fought in the Confederate army, though some were pressed into support work.)

The impact of our war in Vietnam still lives in many Americans alive today. Can you imagine the impact of a war whose cost in Southern deaths was one hundred and seventy times that of Vietnam's? How many men in an 1866 Southern town were simply gone? Little wonder that the South's grief lasted so long and, in some ways, still lasts.

South Carolina, where much of this book is set, led the Confederacy in ways chronological and horrible. It was the first state to leave the Union. Meeting in Columbia in December of 1860, the secession convention voted unanimously to secede. The delegates were wealthy: of the 169 delegates, 168 owned slaves. The war's first shots of the war were fired by Carolinians, when they shelled Fort Sumter in Charleston Harbor.

197

By most estimates, the price it paid in that war led all states. The price is hard to quantify exactly. The numbers in the historical records vary, sometimes because of definition of death. Was a soldier killed in battle, did he die a month later from his wounds, did he die from malaria or other disease? And many of the Confederacy's records were destroyed in the war, so numbers have been reconstructed from various sources.

No matter how you tabulate the price, it was horrific. The most conservative number says 12,922 South Carolinians, 23% of the state's white males of fighting age, died. Other numbers say it was over 30%. Neither of these estimates include the men who were incapacitated, which probably doubles that percentage.

The primary focus of this book is the enduring impacts of slavery and the Civil War on the South, particularly South Carolina, but those impacts were not—are not—limited to the South. War deaths among soldiers from New York, Illinois and Ohio equaled or exceeded deaths from any of the Southern states. However, due to the larger populations of those Northern states, the percentage impact was far lower, with Illinois' 1.8%, for example, dwarfed by the impact on South Carolina.

I'm finishing this book in a time of daunting national challenge. In the name of "Making America Great Again," a segment of the Republican Party is attempting to return the country to an earlier era. Extremists in that party have painted dire consequences if the "return" isn't successful.

In late July, Ohio state senator George Lang, after leading a chant of "fight, fight, fight," told an audience: "I believe wholeheartedly Donald Trump and Butler County's JD Vance are the last chance to save our country politically. I'm afraid if we lose this one, it's going to take a civil war to save the country, and it will be saved."

Lang is certainly an outlier with his willingness to consider civil war, but the party's ultimate purpose, of course, is simply to

198

return to power. Central to that return is reducing the voting power of Black citizens, who overwhelmingly vote Democratic. Their primary tools, redistricting and culling voters from voter lists, are more subtle than lynching and terrorism, but they are effective.

How effective? Is their effect more powerful than the curve of history that blended cotton, money and power to drive our country into civil war? Powerful that curve was. In the decades before the war, the South produced 80 percent of the world's cotton, with half the country's slaves working that crop. Cotton remained the US' most valuable export until 1937. Is it powerful enough to overwhelm the cumulative efforts of men and women who sacrificed and struggled, some giving their lives, to bring our country's actuality closer to its stated ideals?

Numbers demonstrate the power of that cotton-driven curve. The number of enslaved people in our country grew from 700,000 in 1790 to 4 million in 1860. The value of those 4 million slaves was $4 billion, more than the value of everything else—land, homes, factories, equipment—in the South. They were the largest single financial asset in the entire U.S. economy, worth more than all manufacturing and railroads combined. In today's dollars, that equates to $13 trillion.

Future elections will reveal their effect, but recent history shows the Republicans' "return" will be fighting **changes** that have taken place in law, in customs, and in people's hearts.

Change is shown in Elwin Wilson.

In 2009, Mr. Wilson called The Rock Hill Herald to say that he was one of the men who had led the bus station beating and that he had committed other violent acts — against, among others, civil rights workers holding lunch counter sit-ins. Only then did Mr. Wilson learn that one of his victims, John Lewis, was now a congressman.

He traveled to Washington and met with Lewis, who quickly expressed his forgiveness. Interviewed later, Lewis said, "He started crying, his son started crying, and I started crying." The two men made a handful of appearances together over the next two years, including one on the Oprah Winfrey show, and received awards from groups that promote social reconciliation and forgiveness.

In an interview, Mr. Wilson told CNN, "Well, my daddy always told me that a fool never changes his mind and a smart man changes his mind. That's what I've done and I'm not ashamed of it."

Change is shown in Rock Hill's government.

Invited to speak at Winthrop University in 2002, Congressman Lewis was given the key to the city. In 2008, he spoke at Rock Hill's Martin Luther King Day observance, where Mayor Doug Echols apologized on the city's behalf for the Freedom Riders' treatment.

In 2015, Judge John C. Hayes III, nephew of the judge who sentenced the Friendship Nine to the York County chain gang, overturned the convictions of the nine, stating: "We cannot rewrite history, but we can right history." At the same occasion, Prosecutor Kevin Brackett apologized to the eight men still living, who were in court. The men were represented at the hearing by Ernest A. Finney, Jr., the same lawyer who had defended them originally. Mr. Finney subsequently went on to become the first African-American Chief Justice of the South Carolina Supreme Court since Reconstruction.

Change is shown in the dance of love and law.

Early Virginia history includes a famous example of interracial marriage as, in 1614, tobacco planter John Rolfe married Matoaka (Pocahontas,) the daughter of a Powhatan chief. That tolerance was either unusual, short-lived, or both, for in 1691 both Maryland and Virginia banned such marriages. Bans were still on the books of 29 states in 1924.

How appropriate that the 1967 Supreme Court decision that put the nail in such bans was named *Loving v. Virginia*. But old ways die hard. Many states kept their bans in place, despite their unenforceability. South Carolina's wasn't overturned until 1998. Alabama, the last, followed two years later. But even in 2000, 40% of Alabamans voted to keep the ban in place. 25 of the state's 67 counties voted to retain it.

To say that Alabama and Carolina lagged national trends is an enormous understatement. In 1958, the first year pollsters measured attitudes toward interracial marriage, less than 5% of Americans approved. Today, that rate is 94%. Interracial marriages mirrored that approval, with the percentage of such weddings climbing from 3% to 16% of total new marriages over the same period.

The Free City of New York

The more I read the history of American slavery and its consequences, the more I'm overwhelmed with its impact. It started small in the 1600s, as America adopted a practice which was still approved or at least tolerated through much of the world. By happenstance—America's huge inventory of fertile land and its promise of profit—slavery grew through the 1700s and exploded in the 1800s as rice and cotton, particularly cotton, made men rich and powerful.

That trend, a disease increasingly embedded in our fabric, was almost unstoppable. It took the civil war to bring it to an end.

We tend to view slavery and racial bias as either/or institutions, South versus North, but that's an oversimplification. Much of Congress' attention in the 1840s and 50s was focused on whether the new lands of the West would permit slavery. That debate, sometimes violent, raged many places.

In early January 1861, just days after South Carolina announced it was leaving the Union, before any other state joined it and months before Abraham Lincoln took office, New York City Mayor Fernando Wood proposed that New York City should secede from the Union, too. His motive was clear: the city was the center of the very profitable trans-Atlantic cotton trade

Addressing New York's Common Council, he called for creation of a "Free City" of New York, declaring that "a dissolution of the Federal Union is inevitable" and that the city had "friendly relations and a common sympathy" with the "Slave States." According to historian Heather Cox Richardson, he complained bitterly about the taxes the Republican legislature had levied, claiming it was plundering the city to "enrich their speculators, lobbyists, and Abolition politicians." He claimed the city had lost the right of self-government. If it broke off from the United States, he argued, the city could "live free from taxes, and have cheap goods...."

In an excellent example of an argument that rages today—to what extent does regulatory power reside in American cities, American states, or in the country as a whole?—in 1861 Congress passed a federal draft, taking enrollment of soldiers away from the states and giving that power to the United States. Because the Supreme Court had decided in 1857 that Black men were not citizens, they were not included in the draft. New York City's Democratic leaders, led now by Mayor George Opdyke, railed against the federal government and its willingness to slaughter white men for colored people.

New Yorkers responded with the worst riot in American history. The first draft lottery was held on July 11. On the morning of July 13, Democrats attacked federal draft officers with rocks and clubs. Rioters then spread through the city, burning the homes and businesses of prominent Republicans. After burning the Orphan Asylum for Colored Children, they hunted down individual colored men, beating 12 to death before attacking a cart driver who stumbled into their path after putting up his horses. Several hundred men and boys beat him to death, then hanged him and set fire to the body.

Though the rioters thought they represented the will of the American people, they found themselves confronted by U.S soldiers, including a number from New York. The soldiers had come straight from the battlefields to help put down the riots. By the time they were squelched four days later, at least 119 people were dead, another 2,000 wounded. Rioters destroyed between $1 and $5 million in property including about fifty buildings and two churches. In today's dollars, that would be between $20 million and $100 million in damage.

1946

Tens of thousands of veterans returned home as World War II ended. Despite having served their country in the military, colored veterans found the racial climate in Carolina unchanged.

Isaac Woodard Jr., a Winnsboro native, was among the returning vets. Hours after his discharge in Augusta, Georgia in February of 1946, Woodard, in his Army uniform, was forcibly removed from a bus in Batesville, South Carolina. Claiming he was drunk, the Batesville police beat him and gouged his eyes with nightsticks. The following morning the local judge found him guilty of drunk and disorderly and fined him fifty dollars.

Woodard ended up in a hospital in Aiken, South Carolina, permanently blind. By the Fall of that year, his story got press coverage and the attention of the NAACP, which brought it to the attention of President Harry Truman. Truman, enraged that Carolina officials had ignore the case for seven months, ordered a federal investigation.

Lynwood Shull, the Batesville police chief, was charged in federal district court with violations including "the right...not to be beaten and tortured by persons exercising the authority to arrest." On November 5, after 30 minutes (some papers say 15) of deliberation, the all-white jury found Shull not guilty on all charges. The courtroom broke into applause upon hearing the verdict.

Freedom Summer

In 2018 I toured of some of the sites that are memorable in the civil rights movement. Among those places was the Philadelphia,

Mississippi gravesites of Michael Schwerner, James Chaney, and Andrew Goodman, young men who'd volunteered to work registering voters in Mississippi in 1964's Freedom Summer.

During that ten-week project:
- ➤ 1,062 people were arrested (out-of-state volunteers and locals)
- ➤ 80 Freedom Summer workers were beaten
- ➤ 37 churches were bombed or burned
- ➤ 30 Black homes or businesses were bombed or burned
- ➤ At least 3 Mississippi blacks were murdered because of their support for the Civil Rights Movement

Our tour bus driver made sure to get us back to our motel before dark. He didn't want us to be on Mississippi roads after dark.

In 2018!

More on the War's Horror

All wars are filled with horror. The emergence of more deadly weapons such as repeating rifles combined with obsolete military tactics meant our civil war overflowed with it.. Here are some horrific details the book doesn't include, at least not directly.

> ➤ Over 40% of the war dead—North and South—were buried unidentified.
> ➤ With 50,000 fatalities, the three-day battle at Gettysburg was the most costly in U.S. history.
> ➤ In that battle, the 26th North Carolina, hailing from seven counties in the west of the state, lost 714 of 800 men.
> ➤ The 24th Michigan fought the 26th North Carolina there and lost 362 of 496 men.

205

> Nearly the entire student body of Ole Miss—135 of 139—enlisted in Company A of the 11th Mississippi. Company A suffered 100% casualties in Pickett's Charge.

> In 1862, a federal burial detail discharged their duty by throwing 58 Confederate bodies down a farmer's well.

> Equines—horses, mules and donkeys—paid a worse price than humans. In addition to those killed by bullets and artillery, their status as a tool of war equated them to the function of a jeep in today's wars.
> *If it's not of immediate use, destroy it so the enemy can't use it.*
> Between 1 and 3 million equines were killed in the war.

Much of this story is set in and around Rock Hill, South Carolina. The 1860 census of York County district, where Rock Hill is located, indicates half of the district's 21,800 residents were slaves, integral to local cotton production. There were 4,379 white males in the district. They established Confederate cavalry and artillery units and fourteen infantry companies. 805 of these men died in the war. Hundreds more were wounded.

The maxim that time heals all wounds is probably true, but history shows the healing is slow. The great-grandparents of many Americans alive today, Northerners and Southerners, fought in and suffered through this war, and related that suffering to their children and grandchildren. Those stories fuel the persistence of bitterness.

The 1876 Gubernatorial Election
Writing this book required reading lots of history. As a result, all of the book's settings and events are accurate, though some have been modified to fit the plot. A fairly complete list of that reading, some read for fact, some for flavor, is in the bibliography. Some of that reading, while fascinating and instructive, wasn't appropriate for

inclusion in the Story section of the book. Here are a few of such segments.

During Wade Hampton's 1876 campaign for South Carolina governor against incumbent Daniel Chamberlain, he spoke at the Winnsboro fairgrounds. At the end of his speech, which ridiculed Chamberlain's Reconstruction policies, he stepped into the audience and took the hand of a pretty young white woman wearing a dress labeled "South Carolina" and fettered with cardboard chains. He led her back to the speaker's platform and, to the thundering cheers of several hundred RedShirts, ripped the chains from her. The RedShirts were active in most counties in both Carolinas and followed Hampton's campaign through the state, punctuating his speeches with the shouted slogan: "Hurrah for Hampton".

The official 1876 election count proclaimed Hampton governor by the slim statewide margin of 1100 votes, but the count's honesty was bitterly disputed on multiple grounds. In Edgefield and Lauren counties, Hampton's vote total exceeded the number of registered voters. The state was divided, literally, with Hampton and Chamberlain both claiming the governorship. Democratic and Republican representatives met in separate assemblies, both asserting to be the state's government. The Board of State Canvassers refused to certify the election results. The state's supreme court held them in contempt and threw the Board in the Richland County jail.

On November 28, with violence likely, federal troops were ordered to the South Carolina State House to prevent violence. In March of 1877, Hampton and Chamberlain traveled to Washington and met with just-elected President Rutherford B. Hayes. As part of a national Democratic compromise, Hayes withdrew federal troops and Hampton was declared governor.

Croton oil
One of the tactics the RedShirts used in Winnsboro, South Carolina to

damage Republican turnout and influence was chemical. Croton oil is a very powerful laxative. In sufficient dose, it can scarify your intestines, even kill you. A century later, during World War II, the US Navy added croton oil to the alcohol which powered torpedoes to prevent sailors from drinking it. Sailors devised crude stills to get the oil out of the alcohol.

Thomas Campbell, freed when the Civil war ended, was 82 in 1937 when he was interviewed by the New Deal's WPA.

Does I 'member 'bout de red shirts? Sure I does. De marster never wore one. Him get me a red shirt and I wore it in Hampton days. What I recollect 'bout them times? If you got time to listen, I 'spect I can make anybody laugh 'bout what happen right in dis town in red shirt days.

One time in '76. de democrats have a big meetin' in de Winnsboro court house in April. Much talk, last all day. What they say or do up dere nobody know. Paper come out next week callin' de radicals to meet in de court house fust Monday in May. Marster Glenn McCants, a lawyer, was one of old marster's sons. He tell me all 'bout it.

De day of de radical republican meetin' in de courthouse, Marster Ed Ailen had a drug store, so him and Marster Ozmond Buchanan fix up four quart bottles of de finest kind of liquor, wid croton-oil in every bottle. Just befo' de meetin' was called to order, Marster Ed pass out dat liquor to de ringleader, tellin' him to take it in de courthouse and when they want to 'suade a nigger their way, take him in de side jury rooms and 'suade him wid a drink of fine liquor. When de meetin' got under way, de chairman 'pointed a doorkeeper to let nobody in and nobody out 'til de meetin' was over, widout de chairman say so.

They say things went along smooth for a while but directly dat croton-oil make a demand for 'tention. Dere was a wild rush for de door. De doorkeeper say 'Stand back, you have to 'dress de chairman to git permission to git out'. Chairman rap his gavel and say, 'What's de matter over dere? Take your seats! Parliment law 'quire you to 'dress de chair to git permission to leave de hall'. One old nigger, Andy Stewart, a ringleader shouted: 'To hell wid Parliment law, I's got to git out of here.' Still de doorkeeper stood firm and faithful, as de boy on de burnin' deck, as Marster Glenn lak to tell it.

One bright mulatto nigger, Jim Mobley, got out de tangle by movin' to take a recess for ten minutes, but befo' de motion could be carried out de croton-oil had done its work. Half de convention have to put on clean clothes and de courthouse steps have to be cleaned befo' they could walk up them again.

Campbell's wearing a red shirt "in Hampton days" is one of numerous stories of slaves and ex-slaves wearing clothing that symbolized the social and economic status of Blacks and Whites in that era. In another WPA interview, Ed Barber relates some of the motivation for a black man to wear a red shirt.

"Them red shirts was de monkey wrench in de cotton-gin of de carpet bag party. I's here to tell you. If a nigger git hungry, all he have to do is go to de white folk's house, beg for a red shirt, and explain hisself a democrat. He might not git de shirt right then but he git his belly full of everything de white folks got, and de privilege of comin' to dat trough sometime agin."

Described by the interviewer as a "bright mulatto," Barber avoided directly answering a question about his parentage:

"I was born twelve miles east of Winnsboro, S. C. My marster say it was de 18th of January, 1860. My mother name Ann. Her b'long to my marster, James Barber. Dat's not a fair question when you ask me who my daddy was. Well, just say he was a white man and dat my mother never did marry nobody, while he lived.

209

Southern Wealth from Slavery

Like most wars, our civil war was driven by money, by the men (and in those days men ruled the roost) whose continued wealth depended on continuing the system. In the decades preceding the war, a small number of wealthy men developed enormous political power.

In 1861, nearly 50% of the South's income went to 1000 families. The list below is compiled from the 1860 United States Slave Census Schedule. Focused on the largest slave owners, it's far from complete, and the numbers are understated. Some records said "more than 1000 slaves." There's no record of how many more.

South Carolina
13 Plantation owners, 7664 slaves

Col. Joshua John Ward of Georgetown: 1,130 slaves.
William Aiken of Colleton: 700 slaves.
Gov. Robert Francis Withers Allston of Georgetown: 631 slaves.
Joseph Blake of Beaufort: 575 slaves.
Arthur Blake of Charleston: 538 slaves.
John J. Middleton of Beaufort: 530 slaves.
Daniel Blake of Colleton: 527 slaves.
J. Harleston Read of Georgetown: 511 slaves.
Charles Heyward of Colleton: 491 slaves.
R. F. W. Allston, Georgetown: 631 slaves
Wade Hampton (Governor,) 5 plantations, 10,000 acres, 900 slaves
James Henry Hammond (Governor, Senator), 14,000 acres, 300 slaves
Dr. William Weston Adams and his heirs, (now Wavering Place,) Columbia, 25,000 acres, 200 slaves

Mississippi
6 Plantation Owners, 3305 slaves

Dr. Stephen Duncan of Issaquena: 858 slaves.
John Robinson of Madison: 550 slaves.

J. C. Jenkins of Wilkinson: 523 slaves.

Jefferson Davis , President of the Confederate States: 74 slaves on Brierfield Plantation

Joseph Davis, eldest brother of Jefferson Davis: 300 slaves

Stephen Duncan, 14 plantations; 1,000 slaves, cotton and sugar cane

Louisiana
10 Plantation Owners, 5873 slaves

John Burneside, Ascension plantation: 753 slaves; Saint James plantation: 187 slaves. Sugar

Meredith Calhoun, Rapides plantation : 709 slaves; Sugar and cotton

Gov. John L. Manning, Ascension: 670 slaves; Sugar.

Col. Joseph A. S. Acklen, West Feliciana: 659 slaves, 6 cotton plantations.

Alfred V. Davis, Concordia: 500+ slaves, 4 Cotton plantations.

O. J. Morgan, Carroll: 500+ slaves, 4 Cotton plantations.

Levin R. Marshall, Concordia plantation: 248 slaves; Madison plantation, 236 slaves; Cotton.

D. F. Kenner, Ascension: 473 slaves; Sugar.

R. R. Barrow, Lafourche plantation: 74 slaves; Terrebonne plantation: 399 slaves; Sugar

Mrs. Mary C. Stirling/Sterling, Pointe Coupee plantation: 338 slaves, Sugar. West Feliciana plantation: 127 slaves; Cotton.

Alabama

Jerrett Brown, Sumter, 540 slaves.

Arkansas

Elisha Worthington, Chicot, 529 slaves.

Georgia

Jno. Butler, McIntosh, 505 slaves.

Bibliography

Freedom riders, 1961 and the struggle for racial justice: Arsenault, Raymond.

The war the women lived, female voices from the Confederate South: Sullivan, Walter

A people's history of the United States: Zinn, Howard,

A people's history of the Civil War, struggles for the meaning of freedom: Williams, David,

Seasons of war, the ordeal of a Confederate community, 1861-1865: Sutherland, Daniel E.

Mary Chesnut's Civil War: Chesnut, Mary Boykin Miller

Sherman's march: Davis, Burke

South to America, a journey below the Mason-Dixon to understand the soul of a nation: Perry, Imani

Cotton and Race in America: Dattel, Eugene R

Gone with the Wind: Margaret Mitchell

Reconstruction, America's unfinished revolution, 1863-1877: Foner, Eric,

I Saw Death Coming: The History of Terror and Survival in the War against Reconstruction; Kidada E. Williams

Through the Years in Winnsboro: Katharine Theus Obear

Voices of the Civil War -- Charleston (Time-Life Books)

Confederate Reckoning: Stephanie McCurry

West from Appomattox: Heather Cox Richardson

The History of Cotton: South Carolina Cotton Museum

Sherman's March Through the Carolinas: John G. Barrett

Robert E. Lee and Me: Ty Seidule

Waging a Good War: Thomas E. Ricks

Stories of Struggle: Claudia Smith Brinson

Buses Are A-Comin': Charles Person

Incidents in the Life of a Slave Girl: Harriet Jacobs

Andersonville: MacKinlay Kantor

Acting White, the ironic legacy of desegregation: Stuart Buck

Passing. when people can't be who they are: Brooke Kroeger

The false cause, fraud, fabrication, and white supremacy in Confederate memory: Adam H. Domby

The Mind of the South: W.J. Cash

Splendid failure, postwar Reconstruction in the American South: Michael W. Fitzgerald.

The undertow, scenes from a slow civil war: Jeff Sharlet.

Parting the Waters, America in the King Years: Taylor Branch

Civil War Soldiers: Reid Mitchell

Interview with James Peck: October 26, 1979, gathered as part of **Eyes on the Prize: America's Civil Rights Years** (1954-1965). Produced by Blackside, Inc. Housed at the Washington University Film and Media Archive, Henry Hampton Collection.

Made in the USA
Columbia, SC
02 October 2024

42857380R00117